The Red Zone Speeches

Jeremy Rafuse

First published in 2025 by Blossom Spring Publishing
The Red Zone Speeches
Copyright © 2025 Jeremy Rafuse
ISBN 978-1-0684329-2-7
E: admin@blossomspringpublishing.com
W: www.blossomspringpublishing.com

In memory of my grandparents,
Margaret and H. Allan Johnston.

CONTENTS

BOCA RATON

The sliding glass door is slightly ajar, leading to a narrow cement balcony that overlooks a sleepy, palm-lined street full of big, mostly American cars.

The walls are covered with writing awards and an inordinate touch of sports memorabilia. There's a signed photograph of Serena Williams. The floor is covered with NHL pucks and PGA balls.

At Florida State, and later Columbia, I studied journalism. I wrote sports cover for the *Columbia Mirror*. Every day of the week there is a game to cover (the Yankees, Mets, Knicks, Nets, Rangers, Islanders), but spicing up a box score starts to take its toll. Long nights. And sometimes cracking into a beer interferes with the local greasy spoon breakfast special. I decided to go freelance and write about sports every so often.

Just being on the fringes of pitching a deal is more than I could ask for.

I cannot stop flapping an email from Sterling Publishing in my hand. I take long drags off my cigarette. Next, a shot of peppermint schnapps. I begin to type like a grizzled old hack.

Dear Mr. Fisher,

I was asked to write an article on some unsolved murders in Brooklyn. Some cops were said to be on the take, putting collars on the milkman who shows up at the scene of a crime two weeks later. I bumped into an old college friend, who had just come from a Hunter Adamson show. A few pints later, I decided to go to Canada and cover a football story.

It turns out Hunter Adamson's nephew, Angel Adamson, is some kind of football phenom. He ended up dead, near Rouen, France, dangling from a bridge. But here it is: he would have made innumerable *SI* covers, with that easy smile.

Cordially,
Tony

Dear Anthony,

Write it as a novel, and we'll change the names. We'll send over the contract this afternoon.

Cordially,
Mr. Fisher

WINNIPEG

This book is dedicated to the memory of Angel Adamson.

Born: 1995 01 09, Winnipeg, Man., Canada; Died: 2018 02 12, Rouen, France.

Age: 23

"If you're not *in* the parade, you *watch* the parade. That's life."

Mike Ditka, Chicago Bears.

I first visit Winnipeg in late August, 2019, and stay until the middle of October. I return in January. In between, I make stops in South Bend, Indiana, Los Angeles and New York City. I finish the tour in Europe: London, Paris and Rouen.

There's nothing unique about Winnipeg, save a few decent burger joints. I have the pleasure to meet Angel's friends and family, coaches and teachers. I feel like Dr. Phil during my stay. It takes a village to make a quarterback.

The city has a pretty shoddy past. In 1870, Manitoba joins the Confederation of Canada and becomes the fifth province of Canada. Yet the events surrounding the inauguration are controversial. A dispute erupts between glowing Eastern settlers and the Métis. Later, Louis Riel, the hard-bitten Métis leader, escapes persecution and moves to the USA. He later returns to Canada and studies Catholicism in Quebéc. Once more he travels to the USA, where he ends up in Colorado and works in politics. He returns to Canada to lead the Métis in the Red River

Rebellion. He is arrested and tried for treason. Soon after, he dies by hanging.

Winnipeg is one of the most populous Aboriginal cities in the world. However, the disregard for Aboriginal peoples is very pronounced in Winnipeg; the systemic poverty is sometimes disturbing to see. For an Aboriginal person, Winnipeg can at times feel like an exciting place to live: full of successful Aboriginal shop owners, artists, and politicians—but the crime stats tend to dilute any feeling of empowerment.

I lie in bed, surrounded by the strangest orange curtains. The air conditioner is so loud I'm prompted to get up and go to Canadian Tire rather than check out the pool. I notice there are numerous sections of ceiling that have dry spots.

I call my parents. My mom asks me if I'm watching the baseball game. So much shifts in that very moment. My mom always knows the right words to say. To my shame, I forget too often. I put the phone down. The room appears to change color: the TV crackles, the mini fridge is leaking Freon, and the toilet hums.

I focus in on Angel and his passion for the game of football: the most prized sport in my country's psyche, where irascible presidents reveal to the rest of the country that they are real people. Some writers will try and say that football is dangerous or that it's gratuitously violent. But the fact remains: it still tops the list for people who like pizza, beer and sex.

There is Karla, the front-desk clerk, a woman with short hair. Or Harry, the hotel manager, who has a French moustache and is almost impossible to please. The kitchen staff are dislikeable—for any number of reasons.

I come in from the blazing heat. I dance across the lobby, wiggling my toes to the sounds of the air conditioner. Karla exits a gender-neutral washroom, and we make eye contact. I gently hold the *Winnipeg Sun* and search for the perfect line to ask Karla to the movies. I inevitably end up stuffing an aqua-blue fiver into a little plastic box full of pennies.

"I can't believe you love dogs so much!" Karla taps the side of the donations box, indicating she's wearing a new pink nail polish.

"Oh, yeah."

The long stretch of Portage Avenue mirrors the great rivers that converge in the area. Strangely, while you are driving it always feels like you've just missed something. Or it feels like you are in the middle of a windstorm and you're a jostling boxcar.

Crossing the St. James Bridge, it's an easy drive into River Heights. You barrel up a long strip of road, passing the famous Domo and the 7-Eleven, not to mention plenty of nondescript restaurants. More no-name clothing stores. Or, one block north, you can take the more picturesque Wellington Crescent, which offers a glimpse of some of the finest homes east of Hog Town.

Eventually, you arrive at Harrow. Nestled behind the football field stands Kelvin High School.

I imagine a young Marshall, standing in front of an empty TV screen, its surface filled with TV static. He looks at his parents, and then commences to smash the TV box, high and low.

"If I hit the TV enough times, it will eventually appear clear."

Marshall's mother grips the sides of her armchair.

"Sit down, Marshall!"

"But Mother, the medium must appear perfect, otherwise we're all going to die!"

There is a moment's pause, as though Marshall is on to something.

"Sit down, Marshall!"

This is where Marshall McLuhan went to school. Kelvin's most famous alumnus remains Mike Keane. He's won three Stanley Cups with three different teams!

Further along Academy you arrive at Wellington Crescent. A short drive east you arrive at Comox Street, and the famous River Crossing High School: the home of the Mustangs.

*

It is late September and River Crossing is just finding its rhythm on the football field. Mid-row, cars, SUVs, and an inordinate number of Ford F-150s line up along Conlin, Addison, Pennel and Taylorwood streets.

Baseball is probably America's most popular sport in people's hearts. But it doesn't hold a candle to the kind of excitement a football game can create. You sit on the third-base line, squeezing a beer, almost comatose waiting for something to happen. You're a little spooked that you're working on number three. Suddenly, a little flare over the third-base man, who is looking for a double-play ball. You cheer, but it feels rehearsed. You reach for the plastic side of your seat and sit back down.

Hockey and basketball come next. One is very low-scoring, while the other will top the one hundred points mark. Besides, these sports are so combative you can only stand to watch about one per week. Football includes lots of questionable calls, missed targets and turnovers. But when the flash happens—a great rush, a nice catch, someone breaks a tackle—the adrenaline begins to pump. The inimitable characters on the field start to emerge.

Coach Rosen wears a black and gold nylon jacket with the sleeves rolled up, the elastic cutting off the blood flow below the elbow. He's acting a little jittery—rabbit punches from a mickey of vodka.

He knows the playbook better than his kid's birthday. He's preoccupied with his wife Daniella and their silly neighbor, Dylan, one of the Mustangs' biggest fans—or whether the car payment will clear tonight. Football is supposed to take care of life. Instead, he steps up his drink, and starts to hear voices.

Then it clicks: Coach Rosen remembers Angel's asteroid shots from practice.

Angel Adamson has shaggy whitish-blond hair that ducktails at the back. He spends the summer lifting weights, and his arms are muscular. His hazel eyes sparkle in the Indian summer heat.

Coach Rosen searches for something to say.

"Just keep the focus on bringing the ball up the field."

"Got it!" answered Angel.

Coach Rosen squeezes some Gatorade at the ground, and hands it to Angel.

"Because they'll find ways to mess with you," noted Coach Rosen.

"I got it."

Angel takes another sip of his Gatorade.

"We're going up the field." Angel points at the end zone.

"You know the plays just as well as Thomas. I know you're ready for this."

Coach Rosen is slowly retreating from his duties. He is acting like an excited fan.

"We're down 14. But we've got a full half of football. One last gust of wind." Coach Rosen pumps his fist at his side and smiles at the fans.

The student band includes a horn section with a trombone and trumpet, a slick electric guitar, and a tenor with a four-piece drum kit. Local bands have difficulty keeping up with their musicianship. The cheerleaders offer a tumbling routine to match any spectacular play on the field.

The cheap and wobbly stands are more of a distraction than a boost of confidence. A good number of the stay-true-to-your-school, die-hard student body show up—especially if they don't have a test tomorrow. Soon they exhibit a Norman Rockwell demeanor.

A cherry-red Ford pickup finds the high beams, staring out at Walt Whitman's wilderness. The thrill of the game takes over—fans try and leapfrog over each other at the last play; someone spills a concealed beer. They roll with laughter, fuelled by their envy to play the game.

Angel raises his eyes above the green tartan track that encircles the lopsided football field. Thomas looks dejected, unsure what he could have done differently. He flaps his sinewy arms in front of his face.

"You'll be all right."

Thomas takes a sip of his Gatorade.

"Yeah."

"Hold the huddle until you feel comfortable."

Thomas removes the tape from his wrist.

"Find a rhythm. Just stay calm."

Thomas is blinded by his performance. He tries to build Angel's confidence. Angel discards a little grass from the side of his helmet.

"I'm replacing *you*?!" Angel blasts back.

"Forget about it. You've been playing every down from the sidelines as long as I've been here."

Angel reflects on Thomas's words. Angel recognizes the compliment and acts accordingly.

"I got this."

The mostly Grade 11 and 12 students, who play second fiddle, suddenly switch their tune—they are no longer upset at not getting enough playing time.

"Hey, I might play tonight!"

Angel wears his helmet backward and nervously twiddles his black mouthguard inside his cheek. He begins to step away from Thomas's playbook. He seizes the moment. What the fans see, he couldn't care less a less. He'll give them a win anyway.

Angel darts his eyes at teammates, the sidelines, the cluster of spirited fans on the main staircase, the paint chipped electronic scoreboard. He holds a long stare at Coach Rosen. For a moment, the hyped teammates can see a conflict of interest: a domineering coach versus the unknown player. But when Angel shouts a call, he smothers any orders: he sounds resolute.

Angel rocks back and forth and searches out his playmakers.

"Lots of time on the clock. Option. Right. Thirty."

I wear a Florida Gators jersey and watch the NFL countdown show on TSN. I'm hoping to get some good background from Beau and Myles. Myles is of medium build, with thick brown hair, and wears thick silver metal glasses. He speaks in an irritating monotone. Beau is bald with tufts at the front of his crown, which he insists on slicking back. He wears dentures and smokes.

After watching tape, I am ready to do cartwheels. The two knuckleheads just stand, and don't utter a word. There is a disconnect about the importance of a quarterback prospect. Are they being polite? Or maybe they don't want to show up their host? How can you blame them? Imagine the world's biggest trailer park living right under your nose. Just think of how much talent filters out of Canada and ends up the USA. These are the little things that makes sitting inside Tim Horton's, for an American, slightly troubling.

The small media tent is set up near the electronic scoreboard.

"...He looks like a veteran. He's mixing up the plays. He's taking control of the huddle." Beau shuffles his mic on the plastic table, displaying a knot of nerves.

"The O-line looks like they've gained a few pounds of muscle," added Myles.

It's a combination of a good reputation in its own right, nice play action, and terrific footwork in the pocket. Most importantly, it's the ability to see the field. The fans are mesmerized.

Angel looks across the field at the rush of cars passing along Wellington Crescent.

Thomas smacks Angel on the shoulder pads.

"That's what I'm talking about."

Angel removes his helmet.

"The only problem is the option on the left side— because as soon as I take a three-drop the right side seems to open up."

Angel draws a play on his hand and shows Thomas.

"Just take a five-drop, and then flip a dime."

Thomas looks at the fans and can hardly contain his excitement.

A flash of black and gold helmets converges in the huddle. Angel steps back. The frenzy remains: his darting eyes sway from one player to the next, from one call to the next.

He looks at Dylan with disgust at missing an easy block. Or, he glares at Gunther for going deep on the last play, instead of running a diagonal. He includes a little cough for Jack, who is wide open on first down, because he lines up on the wrong side. Angel searches for the one player whose choice of affecting the outcome always comes with absolute dedication to the rules of the game.

They run off the field with a sense of accomplishment. Not a single team in the league can stop the Mustangs' momentum. Angel is not dismayed for the lack of competition. He's tightening the screws, cutting an extra coat of yellow on the up rights, and perfecting his appraisal of the next game.

Madilyn, Angel's mom, is dressed as though she is hosting Queen Elizabeth II for scones and tea. Cameron behaves like he's about to drop kick the gaffer from the local TV station. Angel spots Leah as if it's their wedding rehearsal.

Some of the fans put a few more dogs, burgers, and chicken wings on the grill. The tailgate is now the thing in high school football.

They go over the checklist, but a discerning Madilyn insists they go over it once more.

"Only positive words. The press is half the battle."

Madilyn has no interest in hearing Angel's response. She wipes some grass off his cheek.

"Okay."

"Never mind just 'okay'. Just be yourself."

Madilyn puts on her sunglasses.

The fans glare at the makeshift media tent, with a little surprise that a high school football game can attract so much attention. Angel swishes orange Gatorade in the back of his mouth and spits it out onto the dry grass.

"It's not every day that a player comes into the game and takes control as well as you have," observed Beau.

"In really bad circumstances. A shoulder injury can be really serious," added Myles.

"It doesn't sound so nice to say it," continued Beau.

Angel raises his hand in front of his face to stop the barrage of questions.

"Don't even go there. I came into the game as a backup quarterback, and that's still my role. But at least I showed I can compete and win games," said Angel.

As you drive along the stretches of Academy, Kingsway, and Grosvenor Street there's hardly a heartbeat. It seems like one street crosses another endlessly. You could drive blind, and you'll always end up safe in some mall's parking lot eventually.

Roughly 40 percent of River Heights' population holds a university degree, the highest percentage in the province. During an election, more than 80 percent of the citizenry shows up. All sorts of creative folks are trying to make it big in the world. But there's also a self-deprecating camp who know Winnipeg—and why not check out the West Coast, or Toronto, even Quebéc?

In the North End of Winnipeg, some quaint bungalows or two-storey homes assume a much shadier look. The silence casts long shadows, and the lonely streetlights elicit a more sensational feeling of the unknown. In St. Mary's, the winter-tested homes have less attention trained on the front gardens, compared to those in, say, St. James. A cabbie might have the best seat here, for the city appears so routine. Finally, it's the people and their stories which are of interest to the outsider.

Angel lives in a modest two-storey house with his mom and dad on Borebank Street. Madilyn is a starter on the hard court at the University of Brandon. After her third season she decides to focus on playing the violin. Cameron is no athlete. As a boy growing up in Regina, he is a regular at Taylor Field, and becomes a Roughriders fan. At sixteen he hitches to Montana to see Dan Marino. There are numerous trips to Minnesota, or further east to Chicago, where he sees some of the great Mike Ditka teams.

Sunday is jersey day. Cameron's teams include the 49ers, with a Montana on the back. Or a Minnesota jersey with Tarkenton. Madilyn only wears a Bombers jersey. Angel likes Calvillo from Montreal.

"You know there are pitfalls to the two-sport threat?"

Cameron looks carefully at Angel to see how he replies.

"Yup!" Angel chips in.

"You need to hang up the Air Jordans."

"Shortstops don't come out of Winnipeg."

Cameron takes a bite of pizza and opens a beer.

"We're going to the Super Bowl."

Over on Lindsay Street, Nell hosts a party for the

Mustangs and some of their brash fans. On the strip of CN land, a group of students hang out near a pile of tar-stained rail ties.

Nell's house is white stucco bungalow with a large flower box. The large two-pane front window is covered by a white sheen that glows a soft yellow from the outside. As you walk up the perfectly manicured sidewalk, there is an auto-response to head to the back door.

The basement has no partitions. It has an open ceiling, exposing knotty red cedar, with non-functioning knob-and-tube wiring. The laundry section is in one corner, with a wicker chair and a small metal table. In another corner, a tacky buffet-style bar on rollers. It has a black pleather back and gold buttons and a shiny wooden countertop.

Angel gently directs Leah as they walk through the thick crowd.

"He doesn't look very impressed."

In the main area: a velvet orange couch, and a glass cabinet with a patchy music system. Nell plays mostly old-school rap like Notorious B.I.G., Public Enemy and the Beastie Boys. Free cold beer overflow in a vintage hard-case Coke cooler. The aroma of backyard home-grown weed oozes through the crowd.

Thomas wears dark khakis and retro Jordans, and a navy sweatshirt.

"Just wanted to let you know."

Angel interrupts and points at the bar.

"You need another beer?"

Angel looks towards the packed bar.

"... I'm taking off."

Angel reaches over and scratches his opposite shoulder.

"I got an offer to play in Saskatoon," Thomas states, with a mix of pride and dishonor.

Angel feels the dejection. But soon he takes it as a compliment—because Thomas can win games. That remains part of Angel's playbook. Tonight, however, it's about holding up one's chin, chest out, and ignoring the man. Angel has found a weakness in Thomas's game: an unwillingness to stay, to take a back seat and win games together.

Angel is being anointed the starter. And given the high-status privilege, his first impulse is to hold Leah closer. The little cheers and hoorays of approval show who the team stands behind.

Angel holds his beer a little easier. Soon after, he forgets the name of the muscle-bound young man looking around the room. Just a drunk uniform.

"Listen man, I'm leaving. This is your team."

Angel looks admiringly at the shops along Portage Avenue. The city is half asleep. A gas-station attendant looks a little further up Portage Avenue, welcoming the day. A few joggers. A couple of winos. He parks on a side street and glides over the frosty blades.

JCTX earns a big portion of their budget from adverts for their NHL, AHL and CFL coverage. Angel ingratiates himself around a morning talk-show table. He handles complex questions like a plate of nachos. His ignorance is innocent, and soon he transforms into a curiosity for the early listeners.

"How does it feel to be in the championship?" asked Beau.

Angel peers nervously around the table, full of mics,

or the studio door covered in sound proof foam.

"It hasn't really sunk in quite yet."

"You won the City Championship against Mount Pleasant pretty easily," said Beau.

Angel takes a moment before he decides what to say next.

"Nothing comes easy. I was able to get the ball downfield. I had some good protection."

"They were without one of the more successful defensive backs that night."

Angel nods at an assistant asking for a bottle water.

"We've played Mount Pleasant when they were healthy, and we beat them pretty handily."

"You seem almost disinterested."

"I'm just ready to go. If I can throw touchdowns and bring the provincial title to River Crossing, then I'll smile."

"You are considered one of the best arms that Manitoba has ever seen. How are you dealing with the pressure?"

He gathers momentum each step of the way. No matter if his comments are unrehearsed, or even bemusing and childish—he is being ordained as a football man. He feels the joy accompanying this necessary passage. He greets the occasion as an opportunity to meet new, unrelenting faces, and spread the word that football will pay his taxes in the future. The more he talks, the more he gets used to the football sensibility. He is not trying to impress some prudish English teacher. But he does see the obstreperous kid with a little chip on his shoulder. He fumbles a few words, and frowns at any stream of consciousness. He might be guilty of thinking of Leah. Or the use of some football jargon. But he's free from being pigeonholed.

"Cold brews. Just kidding. I train hard. I work out, I watch what I eat. I do what I need to do to compete better than most people."

"Have you begun to think post-high school career?"

Angel crosses the line, and the boundaries are a little familiar as he goes along. He recalls his mom's advice: let it slide. He smiles and relaxes, and allows some ribbing before he leaves.

"I just want to make sure there's a Porsche in the driveway."

Angel sits on the leather couch in the basement. He holds a blank stare as he tightly grips the arm of the couch. He holds the red power button. He fondly recalls grabbing his Christmas present from under the tall and elegantly-decorated tree. The Santa wrapping paper. He rips open the sides and tosses the paper onto the floor. Cameron takes a sip of a Spanish coffee. Madilyn smiles as she holds Sneakers, a Chihuahua and German shepherd mix, in her arms. Angel feels the hard white strips, and the almost-black leather.

He stands at the landing. He is confused by the candles, a fresh vacuum, and a fresh bouquet of tulips on the table. Marylyn tugs at Angel's arm, and points at the front entrance, where a well-mannered man stands. He wears a light grey tweed jacket, dark pants and a yellow pocket square.

Dr. Smith is the sports director at Northeast Illinois, a Division III school. He has good word that Angel's abilities on the football field can turn around any football program from sea to shining sea.

They welcome Dr. Smith into their home, making sure

he has a strong mug of java and a simple reach to the cheese and crackers and spicy crab dip.

Angel repeats a swing-pass pattern in his head. His palms begin to sweat.

"I asked your mom and dad if we could meet."

Angel smiles at his parents.

"Yup, they told me."

Suddenly, Angel is flung back into a combative game from earlier in the season. He walks slowly away from the huddle towards the offensive line. He anxiously turns and looks at his coach, at the fans, at the scoreboard. And now the wide's at both sides. The team has a confidence that is not typical at the high school level. Yet he is not the cause for the team's success; he is a follower as much as anyone else. He is simply following orders and finding the end zone when it matters.

The offensive line breathes a little heavier than its opponent. The trash-talk back and forth is camouflaged to avoid the referee's attention. Angel continues to ponder why it's so easy to make plays.

Dr. Smith lightly claps his hands to get Angel's attention.

"North East Illinois is trying to rebuild its name. I won't go into the details but there were some irregularities to do with some recruiting. But now we're in the clear." Dr. Smith checks his tie clip.

"Okay."

"We think you are a really important part in the rebuilding process for North East Illinois."

Dr. Smith raises his hands in the air. He looks like he is in some martial arts position.

Madilyn silently urges Angel to speak up.

"He wants to go to College."

"Listen, you're going play in the National Championship

game. Because that's how much we believe in you. I don't care if you're only in Grade 11."

Dr. Smith has given his pitch. The meeting is over. Suddenly, the burden has shifted from an offer to the acceptance. Angel remains unsure what to think.

The kitchen walls are painted a high-gloss white, with a white wainscoting, and pink wallpaper for crown molding. The appliances are polished aluminum. Cameron keeps a pretty tight ship: magnets are not permitted, nor any fried foods in the kitchen—and sugar is referred to as white death.

"He sounded like he was looking to be the next governor of Illinois." Angel takes a chip and a bit of onion dip.

"That's how they talk down there."

The headlines in the local newspapers start to weigh on the games. Angel owns the huddle as if River Crossing is on the hook for back taxes. He has an air of self-confidence that is both alluring and intimidating. He dangles his eyes back and forth at his receivers. He searches for Jaxon, the lanky running-back with good hands, to push off most defenders. Angel barks off a call. He matches their clap. They return to the O-line like gladiators.

The fans don't understand the meaning of special teams. They are only happy when the Mustangs are in the red zone. The assistant coaches have been delegated crowd control. They try and keep track of plays that Angel ends up tossing into the wastepaper basket.

One of the legs of the media tent snaps. Fans giggle as they hold up the tent.

"When did you know you were going to be Provincial champions?"

"When I got out of bed in Grade 6."

I am trying to convince Karla she must attend a movie at the *Towne Cinema 8*. Suddenly, Leah Jenkins walks past. I turn quiet by her impolite manner. Her lack of manners enamors the room; a rush of courtesies and polite smiles and laughter follow.

She has red hair and a porcelain-like complexion. Dark purple lipstick. She wears a black, satin shirt with lace trim. It is very seductive—save the sleeves, which flay and look cartoonish. She wears an inexpensive jean, and brown saddle-shoes. Her red, plastic bracelet is sexy, and she moves her arms gracefully.

After she breaks up with Angel, Leah turns very religious. She refuses to meet unless her husband, Gordon (the title of my next book), and their daughter, Christine, can attend.

Introductions are interrupted when Leah's mom Susan arrives to take Christine home. Susan pushes up the sleeves on her oversized beige wool coat and cranks a wide smile. She gurgles with laughter, snipping several meaningless words at Leah, who is perturbed. Leah is unsure what to say about a man whom Gordon refers to as Lucifer. But, she adds, if she *must* spill the beans, she's willing to do whatever it takes.

Leah stands in the back lane as Angel takes jump shots. He tosses an empty pop can into the thick green grass, which he intends to cut and sweep later. Susan, who stands at the large kitchen window, forces a boring smile—a quick stop back home from her part-time job in the shoe department at the Hudson's Bay downtown. Yet she cannot hide the fact she wishes Leah would date someone with a stronger Christian background. Angel is catapulted into Leah's hopes and expectations: can he carry the burden of marriage, religion, lots of kids? And what about his—very— stale sense of humor?

"I took time off work!" Leah tosses her hair band onto the lawn.

"I told you stuff was up."

"Do you expect me to come down to LA *now*?" Leah looks around, unsure what more she can say.

"No, my parents are going down for two weeks and staying at a trailer park."

Leah turns to the picnic table and shows Angel some pictures from a wedding magazine.

"Really? Look: this is one of the wedding dresses I like."

In Los Angeles, I meet some friends from my college days back in NYC. We go out for chicken tacos, and later walk around the Cove. Maverick Easton, who writes treatments for Warner Bros., asks me why I am so obsessed with death. We enter a magazine shop, and I go over to the photography section. I look over at Maverick, who is busy choosing a cigar.

"I thought I was writing a football story?"

"No one man's life is bigger than the game of football. In other words—this *is* a story about death."

I recall all the beers and cheap whisky. I wasn't having deep thoughts; I was sinking. Football is bigger than death in America. Maybe not in Canada.

*

I wake early the next day and venture over to meet Coach Stanley. I chomp down two egg burritos from McDonald's. I open my knapsack and polish off an airport-size bottle of Wiser's whisky. I pause as I stand outside his tan, poorly laminated office door. Someone pokes me from behind. I awkwardly turn and raise my arms to get some distance. I feel his stubble on my cheek. He digs deep into his nylon pants and finds the keys to his office.

Coach Stanley is bald and has a rectangular moustache and bits of grey scruff on his chin. His thick neck is full of veins. He feels my reach (the proud football man is never off-point). The one who sends Twitter messages to presidential nominees. And hangs out at a few strip bars, where he learns video-poker and says he might go pro some day. His son didn't assault Arron at the homecoming dance; he was just helping out a buddy. ("My lawyer proved that, *goddammit!*")

He discovers I wrestle in high school, and he uses it as ammo to turn us into fast friends: lots of similarities between wrestling and football. Or if we had never met, things would have been different. A wave of hostility comes over me. He doubts my sincerity about writing a fair story. He has some regrets we ever met.

I assume the unmanned garden-hose look. You soon notice a diverse range of opinion emerges.

The well-spoken commando—a former offensive coordinator with too many to name professional football teams in North America, including one in Germany— confirms Angel is pure talent. As long as Angel follows a simple training program, he'll end up in the Hall of Fame.

I take snappy drags. The old-timer, who makes smoothies in the back seat of his Impala— red leather interior—

finally shows me a personal side: greatness is all about how well you fiddle with the pigskin.

I sit in the stands and watch the over-extending, anxious players scrimmage. He comes from a bad neighborhood. Or this young man needs football, so he can support his family. I just need to play semi-professional football so I can eventually get a try-out with a professional team. What happens on the field is life and death.

"Your body is a temple: vacuum, mop, sweep, install a fire extinguisher every couple of yards. Make your body perfect."

Coach Stanley was sounding off. He was his only audience.

After our meeting, Coach Stanley quickly changes to meet his serene family for a Chinese buffet. He'll reach for a honey garlic chicken wing, or the sweet and sour spareribs, topping his plate with three or four egg rolls. He fusses that I didn't care enough about him as a man. His style of speech is like we're always in a live interview. He doesn't have my back, until he's first stretched my face into depths of shit—for not getting his story right. He moans about his back.

He asks me why I refuse Jesus Christ in my life. I'm not unfamiliar with the Church of Latter-day Saints. It is a formidable organization. I tear the aluminum foil off the soft pack of my cigarettes I can see God dripping off his forehead. We share one final cold sweat together before we go our separate ways.

"Angel was a victim of poor conditioning. He should have taken care of his body more. He didn't study how to take a tackle. I'm writing a book on the subject."

"If he'd listened a little better, he would be in a much better position today. And not be some big gun at SXSW."

Coach Stanley decides to run with the ball. He sees me as a by-product of the American culture that he has bulldozed his whole life. Head down, he charges dangerously towards the end zone. During quiet moments, he might acknowledge that the press sometimes makes a valid point, or that his opinions sound off occasionally. But, in the end, those remain items on his playlist that he intends to rewrite. Next, to spit in the face of SXSW, to cut down a sterling film festival—well, you can see how tightly wound he is in American culture. He won't miss any chance to shake things up when he gets the chance.

"I'm writing a book."

"You get what I'm trying to say. Don't try and switch things around. Don't be an asshole."

*

Back at the hotel in Winnipeg, as I turn, I'm standing in front of a live studio audience. Leah and Gordon mope around the hotel lobby. A bank service delivery group replenish the ATM. Karla stares at me while she speaks amicably to Harry. A family dispenses colorful Canadian dollars to their son and daughter at the pink plastic couches.

Leah stands beside Gordon, who talks to a heavily made-up, giggling ex-girlfriend in the lobby. He jokes: we should all get a room. I take my chances and try to get closer to Leah so that we can talk alone. She acts dismissively, and tells me to mind my own business. She tries to play me against Gordon. It may have been

Angel's potential success in football that makes Leah think this is how men should interact. She has a mean streak.

My innocent attempt to connect is really an attempt to sabotage her life. Suddenly, her friend Sacha is mentioned, or that I should be paying her for our time together. Or "find some vouchers" for meals, or why haven't I invited her sister along, when I know she wants to be a journalist? Finally, she goes through her purse and pulls out a box of condoms. She slams them down on the table and yelps *why the hell am I in her face?* She puts on a pouty face and begins to put on nail polish.

She speaks about Angel's trip to LA like it's a second home. Training is commensurate with how well Angel performs in LA. A good throw is how it whistles in the Anaheim wind. Avoiding tackles is escaping a pile-up from bunch of guys from Michigan, Iowa or Alabama.

Angel stares at the massive sign welcoming athletes. The parking lot is bigger than downtown Winnipeg. The estrangement from Canada remains complicated. He knows the American game well enough—the A-list movie stars, all of the Disney characters, fast food, and, of course, the iconic Route 66—and the weighty concepts like freedom and independence. Of course, the history of slavery. Yet Angel notices some trash-talk, a grab at his face mask, and suddenly the tables turn: the dreamy airs of America disappear. Heck, this dude is doing wind sprints after Angel's last head fake.

In mid-August, Angel attends football camp. The camp is composed of highly sought-after players for D1 schools. The staff are mostly former NFL coaches and players. At some point, players need to step back and call family and friends to confirm what they're doing is real.

*

Back in Winnipeg, Angel meets with Leah and brings her up to date with their football plans.

"I was invited to an NFL combine," smiles Angel.

"Okay, and my mom said she doesn't want me to ride on an ATV with you."

"You don't need a licence, Leah."

Angel is miffed how Leah can take some innocent incident in his life—he'd once lost his driver's licence for failing to yield at a railway crossing—and turn it into some life-changing moment. Perhaps Leah likes to get Angel's attention in strange ways, but the overall impact plays havoc in their relationship. Angel tends to react with some astonishment to her indifference, but their future never appears as perfect as Angel would like.

"But you got your licence suspended."

"So what?"

"She thinks there might be a pattern of behaviors, and you're going to get into an accident and hurt me. Don't you worry about other people when you drink and drive?"

July means going to the lake. For most Winnipeggers a popular destination includes the Interlake region, an hour or so drive from Winnipeg, which offers endless summer fun. The name Gimli means protected by fire in Icelandic. Gimli is discovered by Icelandic settlers back in 1875. They land in Ontario, later travel to North Dakota and, finally, by boat through Winnipeg before reaching Gimli. The following year, more Icelanders make the trip. The area includes one mile of lakefront and 42 miles of shore. In the 1930s, farms are converted into cabins. Today, there's a Thai takeout, jetboat rental shops and a realtor's office. Along the wide tree-lined streets with gravel driveways, you notice Pennsylvania, New York, and even California licence plates.

The one-room cabins sit precariously on bricks and run for several blocks. Despite their quaint appearance, they stand as silent protest against aggressive real estate development. The capitalist tendency is to demolish and rebuild quickly. But the ones that hold out, are, when their parents are off-premises, a must-stop for party-hungry Winnipeg teenagers.

They arrive from different schools around Winnipeg: Mount Pleasant, Marshall, Hallsville and Newman: tanned teenagers with lofty dreams. They are mostly eager to get drunk and try familiar drugs and dance. There's a little talk about homework, or even life's difficulties.

*

Back inside the hotel, Leah appears agitated, and begins to push her palms back and forth on her black tights. Gordon doesn't speak. He gets up and goes to Starbucks to get food. Leah stands up and looks out of the condensation-filled window at the traffic passing along Portage Avenue. She clenches her fist and sits back down. Her face changes dramatically recalling the 'incident.'

Leah puts down her beer and politely interrupts Angel, who is talking to some pals from Mount Pleasant. He lifts her into his arms. He notices a mark on her neck. They mingle with friends for a few moments before Angel heads outside.

Some of the more quick-tempered players can't contain themselves and begin to hoot and holler at the prospect of a fight.

"Let's go, Mr. Nigel Stevens!" Angel raises his fists like some famous boxer.

The little green marbles fill his cheeks. Angel assumes the darker side of the student athlete, in possession of an odd propensity for violence. Nigel spends the first bit trying to get any holds on Angel he can. Angel is on his back and is easily flipped (a bear hold is no longer accessible).

Angel runs at Nigel with an upper cut that catches him on the chin. The crowd turns quiet. He throws another uppercut from the other side. This time Nigel rocks backwards, his arm in the air. Nigel is a straight enough shooter to reveal his vulnerable side. His abilities during the fight show Angel to be capable of much worse violence if he does not stop now.

Angel retires, and his shame is widely ignored after some extraordinary fighting. Indeed, the crowd assumes the guilt of violence.

"Oh, I'm sorry, do you even believe in God?"

"Of course, Gordon! Didn't you know that Americans love God. Like, a lot."

The 'church' transforms into a verb. Or it can be used as an adjective. The word can also be used as a preposition, like "we like this" or "we feel this way because..." The church acts as a meeting ground for a surplus of activities growing up: sports, music, theatre or even making movies.

Mr. Lewis stands at the front of the class and talks about the industrial revolution. No sooner, the class descends into private huddles. Suddenly, a slew of ideas is spinning out of control. Next, one student learns that his classmate does not believe in God. He replies with the simple but powerful quip: "I guess you're going to hell someday." For many in the small group it's the first time they have experienced an uncomfortable silence.

He is 6 feet 6 inches tall. He cannot tell the difference between a football and a hole in the wall. He has a permanent ridge above his eyes, like an extra brow, which projects a sense of permanent disgust towards the world. His ears are floppy and resemble mini wreaths of damaged cartilage. His hands are cocky and perverse, but with lumberjack precision, and quick, economical movements.

All of Leah's stories about the past have been affected by her marriage to Gordon. I am a nuisance to them now, more interested in finding the silver lining than seeking the truth. That appears magical to her, except she applies magic potions all day to build a life greater than it was before.

Gordon is none too pleased about offering a helping hand. Yet, his unmatched ability to connect the dots— where sin is found and what to say to move past it— remains intact. Angel, however, is a treacherous sinner.

It's a trap for a lot of non-believers. Gordon could care a less about quoting sections from the Bible. His reactions are as if he has memorized entire passages. Whenever the Lord's name is spoken impolitely, the hint of the slightest stir, Gordon will throw his hot dog across the room like a sniffling child.

He is tired from reading *AutoTrader*. The private sales section does not pique his interest. All the cars for sale say things like: "It doesn't come with winter tires," "Rocker panels need to be replaced," and "New brake pads are essential before you can pass the safety inspection."

Angel comes to the table with a cold three thousand dollars. He has been working as a waiter at Nyra's. He is originally hired to work in the kitchen but gets pushed onto the floor for his "good looks." Vicky offers him a waiter job with the precondition: if he makes it into the CFL someday, he must buy her a house. Angel agrees.

Angel works three shifts per week: Thursday, Friday and Saturday. On Friday and Saturday nights he is out with his friends by 1 a.m.

At our second interview, I break the golden rule and ask Vicky out for coffee. Vicky lives in Kenaston Estates, which is composed of a cluster of town houses, an outdoor pool, and lots of Maple trees. At first, I see a shimmering tuxedo, maybe a purple vest. And laughing at her jokes is easy. Plus, I can shrug my shoulders or point at someone else. Soon she assumes a similar approach towards our 'thing'—but better.

Vicky has more basic knowledge about sports than most sports radio jocks. She is overly experienced in bed, to a ghastly degree. Her occasional retreat from a serious conversation about sports sounds like: "Oh, I slept with him once..."— which feels like a stake in my heart. "Yes, great first down, but I slept with him a few times at some sleazy hotel on Main Street." Laughter fills the room.

Angel and Leah are well versed on late nights. They will always find comfort around some startling alcohol-drenched drama. Inevitably, they say *I love you*. While Angel drives home, Leah sends him heart emojis. Then they sit on pins and needles, fingers crossed that Angel doesn't end up in some ditch, blamed for drinking and driving. The close calls add up.

It's neither frightening nor intimidating, for soon he will act strangely apologetic.

The front windshield is cracked. Angel punches the rearview mirror and it hits the windshield.

"You put a hole through it."

"You think it's funny?" Angel finally looks at Leah, disgusted with lack of composure.

He gets out of the newly washed car and goes around back. Leah follows. His hand is bleeding. Leah cannot stop laughing.

Gordon removes his K-Way jacket and sits down. He manoeuvres his jacket in his arms, like Joe Pesci and Robert De Niro in a blaze of red brake lights, methodical and slightly bemused. I feel what opponents of André the Giant must feel like. Leah smiles in the background. She may have even gone into her leather purse, with the koala clinging to the strap, and put on some lipstick.

Whatever I was doing, I was getting in the way. Gordon answers back: "That's fine, but let's hustle things up today." Oddly, it's not Gordon per se, but the world who has gifted him a sense of ownership. I have no choice but to bite my tongue and oblige. Psychiatry might help. No, we'll accommodate that wish! You are most deserving! Right, dear!

By contrast, Coach Stanley, down in LA—and, somehow, I am just wrong because I am being me. But Gordon goes a step further: he is indignant about the doughnut selection, or that I had not worn a Lacoste shirt to our meeting. Of course, I connect much too easily with Leah. His ideas are dismissed before they hit the ashtray. How he settles with that feeling, I have no idea.

Leah stands by the fence in the backyard. A neighbor hosts a late-night BBQ, which smells like burgers and BC weed. Angel dribbles a soccer ball, and lightly kicks the ball into Leah's little brother's hockey net.

Summer vacation lasts right up until the last few nights of August. Only a trip to the beach quells the overpowering sense of boredom. Friends tend to disappear. Big numbers head up to the lake. Some of the lucky ones go to Florida or California. The ones who stay behind occupy an airy house, make mixtapes, and sometimes the occasional bike ride. Or play deep baseline tennis and of course catch a movie.

Camp is invite-only, and mostly includes quarterbacks and a few receivers. Angel feels the competition on his heels.

They are coming off a championship season. But no one knows what that means, save too much drinking over the summer and not as many spit and polish workouts as there could have been. Who knows when the sense of accomplishment will end. But the wail of praise does not cease, and the echo of *champions forever* has begun to work havoc. Their task to repeat appears simple for most, because of Angel's abilities—but the pressure is making a simple walk look like a drunken stagger.

The competition looks smarter, faster— and a little tougher.

Phil sits at his locker and begins to laugh at Mendoza, who has put too much eye black on his upper cheeks. Angel jumps up and spots Phil laughing.

"C'mon, man. You're better than that! Phil! Are you staying or leaving?"

"Staying!" Phil grabs his football helmet.

"That's right. We've got a lot to be proud about. But not all of you have proven to us you deserve to be here. That includes members of last year's winning team."

"We expect excellence. We expect historical excellence, and we expect every one of you to fight for your own excellence."

This is home to Mount Pleasant Technical Institute. A series of blue metal boxes and the ubiquitous sports medical clinic rest on the sidelines. Fans arrive with beach chairs and set up on the east side of the field. There's a lot of bad blood between River Crossing and Mount Pleasant. River Crossing offers a little more in the way of academics. Kids feel that discord. When the 'RC' is mentioned, tensions rise.

Madilyn hands Leah a little bag of nuts 'n' bolts, which includes chocolate chips.

"Sounds like you're getting pretty serious," asked Cameron.

"We've got lots of time to decide," replied Leah.

There's a little bit of silence afterwords, but not uncomfortable silence. Leah glows at the attention, and even takes a second glance at Angel's parents before replying. She is part of the family. She is playing the dutiful girlfriend role as good as anyone can ask. To be put on the stand, to be asked a personal question, leaves no room to admonish their relationship. Indeed, the murmur of the football game appears to give Leah a rare reflective glow.

"Nice throw, Angel."

River Crossing wins by 50 points. They are being polite. Frank Smalls, the backup quarterback, plays the whole fourth quarter. He fails to dress the score by a single point.

The NCAA is a billion-dollar sports machine, and the individuals responsible for the valuation are called recruits. The athletes play their part, but finding them and getting them into a classroom takes, well, a couple of IBM super computers and dudes who have an instinct for talent.

Jesse Owens, Babe Ruth, Muhammad Ali and Joe Montana are far more valuable to Main Street USA than any other personality. Tom Cruise lies awake at night recalling something he saw on the nightly sports channel. The fact you don't need a law degree to fight at Madison Square Garden keeps the Cinderella story alive and well. We all remember playing a game of pickup ball and landing in the quarterback spot. The Hail Mary. That sense of perfection never dies in America.

Some come straight from the airport. The compact, sporty taxis fill the small teachers' parking lot.

Angel sees some of the recruits at the end of the hallway. They are busy discussing the business of football, no doubt. Angel heads outside and jumps in his car, slumps into his stiff leather seat and lights a cigarette.

Little giggles follow after he reads a DM from Leah, who reckons some of the gents in the foyer (surrounded by colored posters cheering the Provincial Champs) might be attending their wedding someday.

Angel drags his hand over the silver padlocks. Or he peers through the prison-style window of an art class. Moments later, he stands in a shabby denim strait jacket. The unremarkable shop teacher talks about the merits of a career in the trades. Anyone who points their nose at a career in the trades, can be sure as hell that Burger King won't come close to cover the mortgage.

The recruits feel the sting of being out of their comfort zone. They have more in common with Canada than they like to admit: a cousin flees to Canada during the Vietnam war, or they spend a long weekend in western Ontario at a fly-in, secluded log cabin. They sit on oversized silver granite and talk about friendly, glassy waters full of northern pike, walleye, or pickerel.

"Son, that's how we want you to throw when you come to Louisiana."

At one point, they have over one thousand shops across parts of the US and Canada. Who can forget:

Don't cook tonight, call Chicken Delight!
They will fill your appetite
For dinner complete
But, what a treat!
Delivered hot right to your door
Now, I ask you, what are you cooking for?
Why wash those dishes? Don't scrub that pan
Grab a phone and call the man
Oh, what flavor in every bite
Don't cook tonight, call Chicken Delight!

His name is Abe O'Neil. He has blotchy cheeks and good manners. He wears a rakish NASCAR jacket and tight jeans.

He pops the cork of a bottle of Southern Comfort before we can finish introductions. Anyway, he likes Angel. He has him as the next Doug Flutie, but with a whole new set of skills. However, he ends up going off worse than Nicholson calling a Code Red on the witness stand; or else, that Hollywood producer in *The Godfather*, who tears into Consiglieri for losing his star actress. I tend to defend some awkward points when I'm drunk: "Sports are overrated!" or: "What is the point of the Olympics?" He throws the first one. That's pretty much how the meeting ends. "No one messes with Notre Dame. Get it, scribbler!"

Angel agrees to meet Mr. O'Neil, a recruit for colleges in the north-central United States, at most Winnipeggers' favorite restaurant: Chicken Delight, at the corner of Corydon and Stafford Avenue. Mr. O'Neil prefers to meet at the Fort Garry Hotel, an upscale stone hotel on Broadway made in the chateau style, but Angel prefers the ripped red pleather booths and the smell of Mr. Clean and smoky fryers. It's a safe place to eat fatty fried chicken or relax over a tall Diet Coke and crushed ice. The windows are covered in sheets of tinted plastic to keep out the hot sun. The air conditioner feels nicer than a Florida beach.

"So, you got yourself a shotgun. You're not all that keen about running." Mr. O'Neil is a little distracted by how good his hamburger tastes.

"I'm starting to run the ball a little bit more," said

Angel.

"Don't scare me now. We'll let the backs take care of the running."

I host another series of interviews with Leah and Gordon. I order three large pizzas, one Hawaiian and two veggies, when Gordon shuffles over and dangles a piece of onion in front of me.

"What's your deal?"

I offer to send the pizzas back. Gordon keeps rubbing his cheeks and asks how much longer we have to stay. He glances at a watchful Leah to get a free checkup on his mental health. It is blasphemous to discuss Angel's proposal to Leah.

"To rehash the past is to mock God!"

Angel takes Leah out for ice cream. It's rather disappointing in terms of structure: an old boxcar transformed into an ice cream parlor, which includes a hard-to-read sign framed with Christmas lights. It sits on the edge of the murky red river. A converted railway bridge acts as a scenic walk while you eat your ambrosial ice cream. It acts as a tunnel of love for an inordinate number of Winnipeggers, who make the lifelong commitment to marry here.

Angel fiddles with the inexpensive sterling silver ring in his side pocket of his navy cargo shorts. He holds Leah's delicate hand as they approach the middle of the old train bridge. Suddenly he stops, leans against the iron railing, and tosses his pineapple sundae over his shoulder into the dirty river.

"I have to do this: will you marry me?" asked Angel.

Leah holds her cheeks and tries not to cry.

"Yes."

Time stops. Their love is real. Yet, the sense of the fleeting cannot be ignored.

"I want you to go to an American college."

Angel checks for his wallet, suggesting they should get going.

"Yeah. I get it."

The Mustangs have a comfortable 20-point lead.

Frank Schmidt begins to toss the ball on the sidelines.

A little run of play, where Angel goes to the right and the wide comes over to block for Angel to grab a few more yards.

But the defense decides to blitz—and Angel goes down hard.

Wesley Parker has a 100- a-day cigarette habit. Working as a paramedic, his whole being is moderated by incidents and close calls.

His supervisor, Anderson, learns Wesley has left an oxygen tank on his last call: "You *cannot* leave an oxygen tank on the boulevard!" Anderson recalls the most recent incident, where he had to purchase the homeowner a new door because Wesley went to the wrong address. Wesley breaks down the wrong door. He explains to the shocked homeowner he is engaged in a war of life and death, so he'll just have to suck it up. Back at the office, Anderson screams at Wesley: "No one should be required to suck anything up based on your performance in this world."

Wesley drives through the fence. River Crossing hosts a fundraiser to help pay the bill for the destroyed fence. A rather messy time for city council members, as the explanation was to ensure the injured player makes the

NFL draft in time. The principal claims he was yelling: "Slow!" Wesley claims he heard: "Go!"

He lies motionless on the ground. Only Angel is still trying to be a football star, slivering his eyes from side to side. He tries to call a play, or look downfield, push off another linebacker, get some support from the sidelines. But the pain is too much. Soon he looks like a science experiment for the paramedics.

He tilts his head back, at the navy blue, the deepest part of the ocean. The pain flutters in irregular bursts. He gazes at a discombobulated Wesley, at his confusion and dismissal. Suddenly, he's taking orders from some random dispatcher he has never seen before. The circle of pestering eyes, and patches of scruff on their chins. A horny hand comes towards his face. Then some screams. The clouds appear like waves in a huge open water.

"He almost missed you."

"Yeah." Angel gently reaches for his forehead to check if he is still alive.

The slam of the ambulance door. Madilyn and Cameron bicker with each other for a moment. They insist the driver take them to the Victoria Hospital.

Inside the spacious Victoria Hospital waiting room, Cameron acts like a jerk. An ungracious intake worker calls a code white. The police arrive. After a quick negotiation, Angel is allowed to stay.

An upset woman in jeans and poorly fitting sweatshirt sits anxiously, turning apoplectically in her seat. Her caregiver wears a black-sheen track pant and white tee, and has his greasy hair, perfectly trimmed above his eyebrows. Next, the woman leaps up and begins to scream: "You are going to hell!" The caretaker nervously grabs the woman by the arm. Security guards run over and take the woman away.

As he looks around, it is so unfortunate to see someone escorted from the waiting room—he has little sense of the reason for the outburst. Does such an outburst merely represent a polite way to excuse themselves from the room? Here, bound in a sports uniform, a suffocating feeling of white privilege pervades. He pursues a similar exit. The distance from his former teammates seems to lengthen.

Dr. Moore wears a Jets' K-Way and a Stetson. He has a high-pitched voice that seems to accentuate as he tilts his head back when he speaks. He claims he got a few Jets off the disabled list a few weeks earlier than predicted. Suddenly, the moniker 'Miracle' is attached to his name. He seeks out other high-profile athletes, to build his reputation.

He reacts quickly at meeting Angel. He quickly calls his wife and tells her to work the gossip column at the local newspapers. He appears solemn, with the right mix of regret and optimism. Angel remains magnificent. Dr. Moore uplifts the business of others.

"I hear you hurt your leg."

"I think it's my ankle; it's probably just a sprain."

I did a piece for the *Washington Cable*, which catches his fancy. Anyway, Dr. Moore calls me—leaves several messages, actually. On my last day, I go up to see him.

"The best players have a strong relationship with their doctors. That was the part of Angel's game that was missing."

He talks ad nauseum about Angel's spirit. He needs

healing. He doesn't say too much else. He hates that I take smoke breaks.

Angel prods the doctor about girls, politics—and now he finds it hard to dislodge the memory of the young man. He continues to pray for Angel. Angel will be back in no time. Either he pulls through, or alternatively he's holding court on a PGA sanctioned course, ordering people to fill bunkers, and mow the fairways.

This is not Sunday visits: sheen curtains, and comforters with pictures of dachshunds. These are overworked nurses, in $200 sneakers. Half a dozen cigarette breaks; the rhapsodic hum of pill-popping. No one talks about diets anymore.

"Good news: it's just a simple avulsion fracture of the distal fibula."

Angel smiles at the baffle. He scans further down the hallway at some visiting family members. There is a lone patient, who beat his diagnosis, and storms out of his room with a small bag of belongings. No doctor or nurse to help him find the exit.

Angel prepares to leave when a man appears at the door.

Lully Atom is in his forties and appears a little unsure how to act. He taps the cold metal door frame as Angel hovers over his bed, crutches under his arm, and tries to pack his nylon bag with some personal belongings.

"So, is this it?" asked Lully.

Angel looks up at Lully and offers a smile.

"No, no, just warming up!"

It turns out Lully is the boyfriend of Greta Lilly, one of the nurses on the floor. He finds out what room Angel is staying in and decides to come over to say hi. Lully finishes packing Angel's nylon athletic bag and brings it over to the doorway. He smacks the entrance way and runs down the hallway.

Greta enters the room, pushing a wheelchair with white pleather and thick foam arm rests. Angel sits down on the chair. Greta carefully places Angel's bag on his lap.

"What did he just do?" Greta goes over and tidies Angel's side table.

"Maybe he wants to work on as an equipment manager someday."

The Mustangs have one win and four losses since the injury.

Principal Bagby talks to Angel about his injury and inevitably thanks him for last year's championship season. The two men shake hands. Angel goes over to Leah, who sits on the cement stairs and watches the game.

How much he wrestles with his life and how rarely he comes up to breathe. Leah is only partly moved, yet insists she is committed. He counts the days; awaits rehab. He anticipates a more exciting relationship with his sweetheart. They'll travel and build a gargantuan house and have adventures... Their life abounds with gifts.

"Why are we attending a game when you're not playing?"

He watches an overthrown ball. Leah instinctively puts her hand on Angel's knee.

Angel tries to explain, but they are too far apart.

"I am dead to them now," said Angel.

"I just don't understand how you would try and get

ignored?"

Angel takes a double take on Leah. He returns an indifferent gaze at the playing field.

"I don't know what you're talking about," said Angel.

"You slid with your feet up."

Angel opens his knapsack and hands Leah a Mars Bar.

"I was taught to do that."

"You were told to do a baseball slide and you didn't tuck your legs under."

Susan runs into the room and pulls a red cap onto Gordon's head: *Let's Make America Great Again*. I'm rather lost—or I'm Lorne Michael from *Saturday Night Live*, and asked to make a last-minute choice as to whether the skit stays. Now all eyes are on me.

Gordon admits he likes Trump, and wants to know where I stand politically. I refuse to answer. Instead, I explain it doesn't make very much sense to support Trump, given he thinks Canadian Thanksgiving is stupid.

"Yes, he said that," said Gordon.

"Well?"

Gordon curses under his breath and then gently smacks both of his knees and crosses his arms.

"Give it up."

"I'm just saying: he's not anyone's buddy, so don't fall for him so easily."

Gordon doesn't suit glasses. He wears a V-neck sweater with a thick strip of leather around the collar. His jeans are from Denim Warehouse, the style that's put-on clearance before they hit the floor.

"If you mean the detergent argument? Or that stuff he said in the bus? You want me to defend that? Yeah, men tend to talk a little different truth than Hilary Clinton. At least I understand what he is talking about when he talks like that—instead of all that intellectual crud I hear all the time. Let's get on with it. Now."

Leah keeps a diary of their relationship, right down to bad calls on the football field. I ask Gordon about the diary. He replies that Leah needs to be reminded of her past. Besides: "Look at God's willingness to forgive, at some of the nonsense she dealt with."

I want stories that will highlight a little bit of the life of an extraordinary athlete. But Leah has no sense of what that means. That is not to say she does not see Angel pursuing his goals and going a little further than most. But, for Leah, that is still quite boring compared to the baggage that comes with being with Gordon.

I hug the pillow to smother my laughter. He is awkwardly insecure, and refuses everything at the mention of Angel. It's like oil and water. Leah and Gordon prove ruinous to Angel's memory.

It's half-time, and the Mustangs are down a hard 10 points. Angel stands up and stretches his arm into the sky. Leah glances at their car on Wellington Crescent.

Angel draws a play on his hand and shows it to Leah. He feels the itch to play again. Frank is half the player of Angel. That remains an inflated compliment.

After the game, Angel and Leah start to walk back to their car. They stroll through an area built by Charles Enderton, a real-estate developer in the early part of the twentieth century. Enderton wants to put Winnipeg on the map. Winnipeg offers cheap freight routes. Plus, eastern companies can make a big deal with Winnipeg wholesale companies. They, in turn, ship merchandise down into the United States. Enderton builds palatial homes along Wellington Crescent and the streets of River Heights and Crescentwood.

Here's a big, roomy three-and-four-story house, over one hundred years old. This one has a big porch and a lawn as big as a football field.

Angel turns east along Kingsway Avenue, while Leah fidgets, searching for a song to play.

"I intend to lead a team someday," said Angel.

"Oh, give it up."

"Yeah, so like when you don't show up, while I'm trying to get healthy, makes me wonder what's going on in your head."

"We need to talk."

They don't speak and instead stare at someone trying to parallel park.

The trophy cabinet becomes a destination to refuel. He battles grandiose thoughts that River Crossing could have pulled it off without his contribution. Leah taps on the dirty, sliding glass door of the trophy case.

Angel experiences his first Spike Lee dolly shot. He looks down the hallway at the vanishing kids. He turns and looks through the glass door at the passing traffic along Wellington Crescent. He smiles and frowns and tugs at his jug-ear.

"We got together," noted Leah.

"Okay. What are you telling me now? Well, isn't that going to be satisfying when I put Ace's head into the ground?"

"Oh, I don't think he really cares for me." Leah puts

on a little bit of lipstick.

"You will never make the shortlist for anything resembling feminism."

Angel's absence from the football field puts him a little back from the normal trust and acceptance. The once boisterous classroom, with the middle-aged, frumpy teacher in a polka dot dress, or the crotchety History teacher—who wears a track suit and plays with his whistle at 9:07 a.m.—don't appear to be as friendly as they once were. He cannot play for this team anymore. But he sees a playing field beyond the classroom. He is once more in pursuit of Leah.

The student council has set up a fundraising booth that sells Tim Horton's doughnuts, to raise money for teens against drinking and driving.

"Do you want a doughnut?"

Frank cannot deny the situation feels a little tense; after Angel cracks a smile, everyone feels a little more relaxed.

"It is what it is," said Angel.

"Yeah. You'll be all set for next season."

There is an uncomfortable silence.

"Oh yeah, and then some. I'll visit some schools," said Angel.

More awkward silence.

"So, I hear you broke up?" said Angel.

"Subtle?"

"Just coming clean. It's always good to have a clean slate about stuff."

Frank realizes he is no match for Angel. They are not going to fight. Indeed, it's the first time both young men feel pleased how they dealt with a touchy situation.

"Oh, for sure. By the way, I'm having a party for

everyone who helped out with my campaign. So, you got to make it man."

I ask Leah if she is acting disingenuously, given their past together. She glares at Gordon. She doesn't understand my question.

I acknowledge the unconscious bias: I favor Angel's sports career over any of Leah's later choices. I am trying to find the right words to tell Angel's story. But fumbling around never works with Leah, and she doubts I can tell anyone's story. Since her happiness is commensurate with whatever Gordon is thinking and doing, she just stares at him for an inordinate amount of time. Finally, she gets up and runs out of the room.

I've owned maybe three suits in my whole life. My closet includes mostly black Levi's and polo gear, and rugby and Oxford shirts. I've been on the road with the Hershey Bears in the ECHL. I've gone to Afghanistan four times. Some of my magazine work includes *Playboy, UTNE Reader, The Nation, Hockey News* and *Sports Illustrated*. One girlfriend ran for Congress but lost to a Republican. We Googled zip codes and ate pizza and drank Merlot for six months. So, when I ask Leah why she takes an interest in Angel after his injury suddenly God pissed his pants. Gordon stands up and points at me: "Do not speak to my wife like that!"

Angel swoons over the Provincial Champs' team picture and the lustrous hardware. Classmates react in the hallway. Abe rushes over to Angel and gives him a high five. Even Steve, who hits deep threes, sees his chances with Leah fizzle out of sight.

"You didn't tell me you were going to camp?" asked

Leah.

"Yeah."

Leah sticks her hands in her back pocket and tries to look up into Angel's eyes, but he quickly turns away.

"I was just waiting for you the whole time. Well, just so you know," said Leah.

"I know." Angel gives an arrogant smile.

"I'm allowed to do that."

Most of the bars in Winnipeg are connected to some beer store at the back. Sometimes the bars are connected to a shady one-or-two-star motel. To find the hard stuff, you need to go to the liquor mart, a chain of provincially regulated stores.

The Galaxy South sign flashes on the dark street. The thud of a nearby train obstructs the senses.

This is not easy street: you watch your mouth and you check the attitude. Admitting that Aboriginals have it a little worse is the first step out of a hard stare. Suddenly, the drinks pour, the atmosphere turns electric, and the rock and roll create both forbidding and inviting textures.

Angel finds a booth at the back. He wears a Raiders jersey, black jeans and Vans. They play '80s rock, like Journey.

The waitress places two Buds on the shiny black table. He keeps his eyes low. He wrestles for a tenner.

A tipsy assistant coach walks past and notices Angel. The silence is a little awkward: Angel is underage, sitting inside the bar. Quickly, Cliff Netts becomes the quiet assistant with good work habits.

"What is this?" asked Coach Netts.

"I was just meeting my dad."

"You're such a liar. Dude, how old are you?!"

Angel raises his eyebrows, and squeezes the emergency break.

"I'm old enough."

"Dude. You are still 17," barked Coach Netts.

Coach Netts sits down and begins to roll a joint.

"Listen, if someone saw me in here talking to you, we would both be killed. Has the fibula fully healed?"

Angel looks at Coach Netts but really has no investment in their meeting.

"You could always play in Europe."

"I don't think so."

"Germans love football. Plus…they've got wicked beer," said Coach Netts.

Angel brings his tapered hand up to his face and forces a gap-tooth smile.

Susie Silver, the gas station attendant, marries Tom Epster, the centre for the Mustangs. Tom and Angel were close at one time, mostly from bumping into each other at backyard adventitious parties, where Angel practises a no-football-talk vibe. Susie claims Angel comes over one night intending to kill someone.

I visit the gas station. Clifton Learner tips the scale at well over five hundred pounds. He wears custom fit jeans and a baggy tee. The back of his tee portrays a picture of his grandmother, lying on a beach, toned, in her bikini. He promises his grandma she will be famous someday. Just the thought of wearing Grandma on your back and pumping gas all day seems a little odd.

Angel drives along the Lord Selkirk Highway towards North Dakota. He stops at a gas station and parks out back. A view of the open prairie as far as the eye can see. A silver, aluminum silo stands mighty in the distance, reflecting a hypnotic carousel of colors over a wide stretch of snow.

Clifton goes over to Angel's car in the parking lot and gets in the passenger side. Because of his weight he cannot turn and look at Angel.

"I own this gas station. One of the employees was wondering if you were okay. She was getting a little nervous with you in the parking lot, for several hours." Clifton taps on the frosty window.

"Yup."

"Because you've been sitting in our parking lot since, like, 3 a.m., from what I understand."

Angel turns toward the stranger sitting in his car.

"I bought a coffee and a carrot muffin."

Clifton taps the dashboard and looks at Susie's silhouette inside the gas station, serving coffee to a customer.

"Look I'm not really interested in some guy in the back of my store," said Clifton.

"You should have thought about that before you open a gas station in the middle of the prairie," replied Angel.

Clifton lets out a great sigh.

"I know where you're at friend," said Clifton.

"Dude, I'm just dealing with the winter."

Angel remains calm that a total stranger is sitting in his car.

"Yeah, Susie quite nearly called the police."

Clifton lowers his head and flutters a few unintelligible words before he begins to speak.

"This is your little safe place. I get that," said Clifton.

"That's right."

"Do you know what it's like to drive for three hours when an employee tells you they think someone is about to kill them?"

"No."

"Maybe I'll talk to Susie. And suggest she shouldn't overreact."

The conversation was over. Angel was mildly impressed how insane the situation sounded. Angel jumped out of his car and helped Clifton get out of his car.

The physio clinic is equipped with the latest fitness equipment: a vibration plate, power rack and suspension trainers. There are battle ropes, treadmills, a stair stepper. There are several mini tramps, kettle balls, and stationary bikes.

Dr. Moore talks about the merits of Ottawa. He has narrowed his search down to two churches. He intends to enter federal politics. He likes Winnipeg—but Ottawa has more potential.

Dr. Moore is even more sterile than the medical equipment that surrounds him, if that is even possible. But when he speaks about the future, his color changes. However, the perfectionism of his life emits a flutter of doubt, of whether or not true happiness really exists. Dr. Moore is saying that it does. But, as Angel looks up from the examination table and focusses on the doctor's grey shirt, the dishevelled tie; he does not appear like the champion of happiness. Angel reaches his hands behind his back and pushes himself up on the black faux-leather table, thinking maybe Dr. Moore has a drinking problem.

"So, you find federal politics more appealing?"

"If I can wrangle a way to make improvements, then that's what I'll do."

Dr. Moore inspects Angel's ankle and foot.

"Put a little of pressure on. A little more," said Dr. Moore.

Angel looks into Dr. Moore's eyes, unsure what he means. "I'm not sure what the thought is?"

"Is that your existential thought of the day?"

"It's okay..."

"There's always pain as we make progress, because we're reintroducing you to muscles that you have not used in a long time."

The loss of mobility is much worse for the athlete than the actual injury. The horrible feeling of being sidelined. The inability to move is one of the cruellest feelings an athlete can feel. You are at the mercy of seeing yourself as ordinary. Then the call to take steps through the injury, to refocus, to avoid 'that' hit again.

The football guru is finally making good use of his *Mad Magazine* pharmaceutical degree. He's begun dealing Angel Ativan and an assortment of other cocktails. He awakens Angel from the dead. Now, he wants to see the pigskin take flight.

I meet Coach Walsh at Bernstein's deli—one *helluva* lunch (Reuben, bag of Lays chips, and a coffee). Coach Walsh wears a tight-fitting peacock blue suit, with wide lapels. He has an electric presence. He talks and talks about drills, routes, and hand-eye coordination. I hold the coach's iPhone: Angel is unloading fastballs. Back in the States, the indoor athletic park video would get one million hits on YouTube.

They meet at the indoor athletic park. There is a small arcade near the entrance, which includes an eight-ball table. There is a series of old school arcade games like

Centipede, Tron, and *Dragon's Lair.* The cafeteria has an impressive daily special.

Coach Walsh has the D-line up against an invisible O-line. They raise their arms. Soon Angel has them in a four-car pile-up.

"Try the three-drop," said Coach Walsh.

Angel drops back three steps. He looks up field. Next, he pivots right and explodes towards the receiver on his right.

"Now try the five-drop."

He drops five on a diagonal, and then takes one clutch and finds the middle, narrowly missing a snake pit of hands and arms.

"Okay, let's try some routes."

It's like riding a bike: he shifts his head slightly, pumping his shoulders, and the weight distribution is perfect. Angel shifts the attention to the impressive, ambidextrous receivers—a little underthrown, to change the tempo. Or long: admire the vertical leap of the receiver.

To all intents and purposes, South Bend, Indiana, is not the most exciting town in the world. But it's home to the fighting Irish—and that truism is omnipresent on your daily walk. That is: a quiet little block, maybe includes a few mom-and-pop shops, a Subway Sub or Home Hardware. However, once you enter one of these shops, suddenly football is leaking from the ceiling.

We are at some diner on Main Street. You know the type: red leather booths, rounded polished metal, and hot neon signs: diner, doughnuts, soda, pie, cake, meat loaf, milk, rye... There is a carved eagle at the antique cash register.

Mr. O'Neil refuses to discuss the Chicken Delight fiasco. Now he burns over the fact Angel and his parents make the trip down to South Bend (the scenic route). The trip ends up costing him more than had they chosen to take the plane and stay in a five-star hotel.

The waitress balances big orders with sinewy arms and a plastic assortment of flowers on her chest. Don't be fooled: a couple of booths are occupied by a group of Avon lady wannabes and toastmaster champs, steering the new waitress from asking prying questions. It is ruled over by some no-name sports channel that plays reruns of great catches, hits and smashes that keep the world breathing. Or, the old man who sits with his three friends, and his world-famous beard that he dyes black. The high-gloss leather cap, with a thick chain on the brim. Tinted police shades from early '80s Midway boxes. A cute elderly couple in matching dark grey Notre Dame sweatshirts, who speak not a word. Old alligator face, with little blue marbles, and his talking friend whose hands are warn from clapping first downs and touchdowns for over forty years.

The Adamson's stand at attention, straight and tall in the middle of Notre Dame stadium, where Mr. O'Neil looks a little on the supple side. The big, swooping corners give the old place a modern feel. A few specs sweep the popcorn and plastic cups.

"What does South Bend Indiana say to you?" asked Mr. O'Neil.

Mr. O'Neil looks at the scoreboard. He flings both his arms into the air.

"What does Montana and Flutie say to you? Condoleezza

Rice, Regis Philbin? How does the name Phil Donahue sound?"

Angel is starting to see the picture.

"Okay."

Angel feels a little embarrassed by the mention of some pretty important politicians and entertainment people.

"You see the picture I'm painting. But we do football pretty good too."

"Yup."

"You know about the 13 National Championships. You like TV, right? NBC covers every Notre Dame game."

"Okay."

Mr. O'Neil finishes his pitch. He looks around the stadium and enjoys the feeling of a perfect football stadium and building his team, building culture.

"You feel me. It's about culture."

Why not take the free tickets to Notre Dame and run? Besides, Cameron and Madilyn are already in seventh heaven. Or has Cameron got another implausible suggestion—let him play in Europe? Madilyn carefully chooses her words: "Let's just take our time."

Angel pulls at his striped silk tie, loosens the knot, and now wraps his fist like a boxer. He looks at his navy pinstripe leg. Cameron and Madilyn are in a state of ecstasy. Cameron watches Angel more carefully here than he does on the football field. Madilyn begins to feel flush, nauseous, faint, and even inquiries about valium. For the first time, Cameron says, "Hush up, Madilyn!"

This type of man masks anger by shoving his chest against the leather-covered, foam-padded steering wheel in traffic. Some of the wives go along with it. Go along with fancy meet-up groups, and keep obstreperous sons in line with fake smiles and punchy retorts. These wives, with their long faces, become too irascible to evoke a coatroom conversation.

The American dream is alive and well. The Adamson's have Hunter to prove that miracles really do happen. Hunter strikes gold in Regina. Imagine what Angel can do, with Winnipeg as his launch pad. A decent swing pass, nice moves in the pocket, and an eight-minute YouTube highlight reel will make things right.

He gawks at the 10-stall gas station. The feeling is getting real: a chlorine burst, an exotic reality.

"I would be proud if you could attend this school," said Cameron.

"They want to play me as the backup quarter back. They are planning on doing lots of shuffling, but it still makes me number three."

"Oh, heavens."

"I'm not going to sign just because they can afford to sign me. I'm trying to lock an NFL contract. And they are more interested in filling a roster sheet."

Madilyn raises her napkin, and gently folds it and puts it back on her lap.

"Stop!"

"I'm serious. This deal will not help anyone at this table!"

Madilyn wears a turtleneck and grey denim jacket with silver studs. Cameron wears a dress shirt. Angel holds a wry smile at his parents' appearance, a slightly guarded countenance, a wobbly faith he'll make it on the football field someday. Or his face has a glow of red embarrassment: he's suddenly become a commodity. Meanwhile, Madilyn and Cameron make eyes at each other. They watch each other's hand gestures, or the corner of their mouth while they eat. Any sense of perversion is seen as ghastly, for they are united to celebrate the fortune of their son's celebrity on the football field.

If there is only some way to bridge Angel's ideas and the quaint surrounding. The waitress pours Madilyn and Cameron a glass of wine. She offers Angel a glass of wine.

"Are you having wine?" asked Madilyn.

"Can I get a Bud?" Angel crossed his arms, not awaiting an answer.

"Do you need a glass?" asked the waitress.

"Sure."

"She's quite pretty."

"Let's try and eat without making any scenes please."

The waitress returns and rests the tray on the side of the table. She politely hands each dish to everyone, repeating the order.

*

Cameron sets up a computer desk, with wood laminated surface, where they execute high-end business decisions. Angel puts the best US school in one pile and the Canadian schools in another. But the well-disposed search is never a true pursuit. He wants to play in Winnipeg. Moreover, one's football career doesn't begin until one finishes college anyway. Why should he take his talents to UCLA, when he doesn't know California from a hole in the wall?

He puts on about twenty pounds of muscle and owns a PB every time he hits the track. A recruit from Illinois comes up three times this month. Francois Letourneau, the lawyer Cameron hires to help Angel in business matters, begins work on a sponsorship deal. A brawl erupts at Pizza Hut, when Francois is unsure whether a shoe deal will compromise Angel's eligibility to play ball in the States.

And besides, a college career isn't long enough to tell his story anyway. He has numerous other rationalizations to stay in Winnipeg.

Winnipeg doesn't have a Main Street per se, a place where the city converges. Some might argue it is at Portage and Main. But it is far too wide an intersection, and unfeasible for tourists to really take advantage of anything there. Even the Forks, the crossing ground of the Assiniboine and Red rivers, appears daft to most locals. Olive Garden is the undisputed champ. To say otherwise sounds callous.

He paces a few feet. Next, he stops and tugs at your arm. It seems malicious at first, but it quickly turns to trust, and is even slightly humorous.

Coach Walsh plays football at Washington State, as a backup quarterback. He breaks all kinds of records back in Ontario, where he plays his high school ball. He has an eagle eye for talent when it comes to the quarterback position.

He knows the US college game is far superior to the Canadian one. Accordingly, he puts Angel in situations wherein he has to prove himself a little more than usual.

The Western Centre, the Keystone College hockey rink, has a large front entrance, which includes offices and a few medium-sized classrooms. Angel holds the posture of a drill sergeant. He plays hockey at the Western Centre as a kid, or else attends basketball camp here in the summer. The two men like the familiarity, and even try to take that comfort zone to another next level: the university football career.

"Matty gets the start for this year, but you'll get some starts," said Coach Walsh.

"Okay."

"I think we can win four championships with that arm. I expect you'll be our number one guy soon enough."

Angel searches to show some signs of excitement. But Coach Walsh can tell there's something amiss. Angel has not pursued leaving home well enough. It feels more like a demotion than an accomplishment. But they both grit their teeth and admit that this is the right choice. Angel smiles and hollers with joy. He slams his hand into the coach's hand, and they banter with pride over what they have accomplished.

"Can you give a handshake and let's get some commit noise going?" asked Coach Walsh.

Coach reaches inside his jacket and pulls out a green Heineken.

"I'm going to have a beer now."

"Okay."

"But *you* are not allowed to have one."

Angel spots some players from Bottineau High School, Mount Pleasant, and a wide from Willow City High—whom everyone says is the 'big cheese'. Families mingle with their extra-large sons. It all looks so unspoiled. Then everyone takes a collective sigh, at the importance of today's meetings.

"That's Matty. Their number one."

Angel tries to get Matty's attention.

"Just until *you* step onto the field. And smile."

Cameron obsesses about *North Dallas Forty*, a football movie starring Nick Nolte as Phil Elliott, a player for the North Dallas Bulls. There is a scene where Phil sits in a hot tub and drinks a beer. It has meteoric influence over Cameron. The first time a philosophy student hears Socrates talk about justice in *The Republic*. A man drinking a beer in a hot tub, right versus wrong— it's the same as the meaning of life.

Cameron hollers at Angel to come downstairs. Cameron wears knee high socks and polyester short, and white cotton tee with red trim. He is a study in focus and determination; nothing will undermine his attempt to turn Angel into a football star.

Cameron stands in a corner of the basement, which has been transformed into the locker room of the North Dallas Bulls, including a stainless-steel cold tank.

"Just like the movie," noted Angel.

"Yeah, what do you think?" Cameron straightens one of the posters on the wall.

"I think the movie was made before I was born," said Angel.

"1979, in the year of our Lord!" hollered Cameron.

Angel inspects the posters and the replica helmets.

"God bless the North Dallas Bulls!" Angel gives several claps and gives his dad a high five.

"That's right, son. We'll get you to the NFL. Don't you worry about anything!"

The hallway includes floor to ceiling posters of this year's starters. They have a leather couch with the Yellowjackets' logo embroidered on the back cushions.

They want to win the Glacier Cup. But when two assistants walk through the dressing room just to meet Angel, the team quickly adjusts to match the face with the highly-touted name. Now they notice each other's obsessive-compulsive techniques. A preparedness; on high alert. An almost sickening preparedness.

"The last time I looked we had five appearances. We seek out greatness from each one of you. Would winning a National Championship make you feel proud?"

"Yes!"

"Would sharing history with next year's team, and subsequent teams, make you feel proud?"

"Yes!"

"Then find your personal greatness and get it done. Let's have great practice, boys!"

When I was a kid, we owned a decent TV and DVD player. My dad hooked up the stereo speakers to the TV. But when we watched *Total Recall* you'd press 'play' (hopefully the batteries were juiced up). We munched on Kettle Corn or homemade nachos. Neither of my parents took any interest in electronics. The TV was something we kids took care of.

The entertainment section looks like the *Star Trek* bridge. There are three 4K flat screens attached to the wall, even a life-size cutout of 'Neon Deion' Sanders.

"I think I've seen enough." Cameron claps and gives a hard look at Madilyn. We end up at Earl's, and it was literally it never discussed again.

"It's one thing to have a lot of power—and quite another to have touch."

Angel has heard all of these stories before. Indeed, he has seen the Brady footage more times that he would like to remember. This is not a coaching session per se, but rather his dad trying to create memorable moments in their relationship. But it comes off more as Cameron checking out how he is speaking to his son. Given all the attention Angel has been getting lately, his dad's words just end up feeling like extra 'stuff'. Out of respect, Angel listens with undivided attention because his dad is only looking out for his best interests.

"Look at this one from Brady." Angel points at the computer screen.

"Some guys out there are capable of throwing a Hail Mary all day without any thinking."

"Coach Walsh was talking about moving the ball slow up the field. Have a lot of options."

Cameron takes a sip of coffee.

"Always check for the sidelines first. Then check for the middle. If you need to chuck it long… only do it occasionally." Cameron continues to nod after he has spoken.

I rent a banquet room. The former teammates greet one another like it's a class reunion. Jace Adebayo, who lives in Kenora and works as an insurance broker, arrives with his new wife, Belinda, and their newborn baby, Sally. Kraven, who plays slot back on River Crossing's championship team, lives in Brandon, where he owns a small sporting goods store. Tyler, the place kicker on their high school championship team, is newly divorced and works for the RCMP.

Jace asks to speak to me in private. He explains his grandfather once played in the NHL. However, his grandfather was already at the end of his career so it didn't make much sense to call him up. After all those years of playing semi-professional hockey from Michigan to Alberta, well, the call up to play on the third line was more of a dismissal than a compliment. I wasn't sure what Jace wanted me to say. I nodded my head and, luckily, he could see I had my own battles trying to tell Angel's story.

The others come from poor or middle-class families, originally from England and Scotland, and homestead in remote parts of Alberta, Saskatchewan, and Manitoba.

They all say the same thing: Angel has a cannon for an arm and is whip-smart in the pocket. He is already flirting with an NFL career. Angel wants everyone to make it the next level like him. It works to motivate the troops. Angel, they admit, is a natural leader.

Further along Bison Drive you arrive at Charlestown Road. Suddenly, you're in the land of Ferris Buller. Lots of two storey homes, cheapish building materials, and quaint enough for a young dentist and a growing family. Certainly, convivial enough for six or seven hungry linebackers who, over a few pitchers of watered-down beer, agree to buy a house and flip it in a few years. Hosting parties becomes a five-nights-a-week affair, which includes panicky looks at where to buy an engagement ring on Monday mornings.

"Yo, man! We got a lot of hope going into the season. Between you and me, you should be starting."

Angel raises his drink, and smiles for the first time with his new team.

Coach Walsh has a *Dr. Jekyll and Mr. Hyde* character. He has the look of having a side business selling pearl—

and an anti-aircraft missile launcher to anyone who can afford it. But he is also the ol' reliable, or the ol' time principal who sits on the sidelines at the high school dance. He catches an undisciplined student with a full bottle of Jack Daniel's. There's a small chase, and the bottle ends up shattered in the men's urinal. The aftermath results in chilling giggles from the student body. The principle with a permanent twitch, but maintains the dance is a total success: "The best event of the year so far!"

"I'm super pleased that you dudes are good with each other. I'm really proud of both of you boys. It's going to work out. Both of you will achieve your goals. Watch the drinking," said Coach Walsh.

Collectively they are one. The comradery gives them all a little bit of lift. The feeling of invincibility plays enormously in their interactions. The music twists and turns a little easier. The drinks hold color, and a change in their temperament, and their friendships strengthen, together, and "we are brothers" comes naturally. Any debates erupt with quick resolutions.

"You know, I'm downtown."

"Yeah," Angel replies, with a serious demeanor.

"Just put it into drive. Find your flow. But, most importantly: find your brothers."

*

Thirty-five thousand feet above sea level is a patchwork of squares and rectangles in various shades of green. Next comes snaky rivers, and now the jagged cliffs and snowcapped mountains, then more rivers: aqua and green, and silver and black.

The Fraser River inlet cascades into the Pacific Ocean and moves tanker traffic at a pretty good clip. Meanwhile, Vancouverites bask in the joys of sailing, jet skiing, and—with the Rocky Mountains just over your shoulder—another extreme wilderness: inveterate snow aficionados hit the moguls—or carve out big, swooping turns on a snowboard.

Vancouver has a sleepy reputation until the 1980s—around the time of Expo '86—when the city decides it wants to be bigger and better than Toronto and Montreal. The Vancouver property boom takes place. It makes a pretty good hop, but it's been spiralling wildly out of control ever since.

The Pacific College campus is found behind Georgia Straight beside a botanical garden and a farm.

The Timbers are as good as any team in the Western conference.

"You've thrown two picks and fumbled the ball once," screamed Coach Walsh.

Matty doesn't have a very good excuse. But he realizes his career is on the line. That is because Angel is on the sidelines, and not because he made a series of misfires on the football field. Matty looks at Angel and shakes his head. The days as the number one quarterback are hard to let go.

"That was Washington?!" retorted Matty.

"You gave him a terrible hand-off," countered Coach Walsh.

Angel feels the blitz. He makes the D-line try and catch him while he zigzags back 20 yards from the line of scrimmage—before he launches deep for an easy touchdown.

After he returns to the bench, Coach Walsh appears

disturbed at how badly Angel embarrassed the D-line. He cannot stop from spewing, a rather humorous thing to see from a coach.

The ball has some extra lift, a little more spiral, and his teammates are easy targets. The fans are taken out of the game. The field is fluid, with an open path to the end zone. He sees Coach Walsh: oily hair, yelling into his headset, pulverizing his pen and the clip board. Angel continues to take easy looks at the other players on the sidelines.

The huddle works to demystify the plays they have just accomplished. They curse, hesitate at revisiting a bad call, or look on the field. They await one further word of motivation only.

"Nice catch." Angel drops his head and searches for some more compliments.

"Yup."

"Four minutes, boys, might lose some friends on the sidelines… Let's run the option, with slot seven. On three."

Sneaking a peek at the Yellowjackets' logo, Angel takes a gulp of wind and pulls at the collar of his jersey. He glances at the end zone and gives his wrist a little squeeze: the sensory experience of total control. He needs one big play every couple of downs as he goes along. The game pressure is a reminder to take it all in. On the horizon he sees excess, an opportunity.

"What are you trying to prove?" asked Coach Walsh.

"He was one beat short of a touchdown." Angel scratches the side of his face for running the ball.

"Would you please put the ball in the air? And never mind these drops and running plays," said Coach Walsh.

Angel arrives late to the huddle, after he gets a fresh

wristband from the sidelines.

"Hey, boys. We're short on time here—the under three minutes rule is now in play. Swing 23 and pick up some yardage. *Please*," yelled Angel.

The huddle suppresses any doubt.

"Let's go through the middle, ten, on a five-drop. Let's get past fifty and head towards the red zone. On three," hollered Angel.

Suddenly, Coach Walsh changes. It affords Angel to see a little rest-stop. Maybe he is behind Clifton's gas station, an open prairie, a winter jog, barreling down the floodway, crossing the field, busting out the back door on Borebank Street and going to play some football.

"Don't sound so defeatist." Angel sensed he used the wrong words.

"I'm the goddamn coach!"

"We just picked the ball." Angel begins to enter the field.

The O-line is on a blind date, and Angel shoots them down before they reach the front door. They meet in the huddle like long lost friends and cannot wait to prove their purpose. The expectations are to be in the lead after their next collective clap.

"Just a swing, five to make a first, I'm going to kick it to the post if we see room. Stay live twenty-four. Hut," hollered Angel.

The ultra-talented, elite athletes share in their commitment to winning. Any weakness in their game is actually quite thrilling to notice, for no sooner does one appear than a vivacious, energetic player will make a spectacular play. They are bored with failure; they are dedicated at becoming great. It's hypnotic towards a single pursuit, and the leaders are admired, ultra-resplendent.

The choice to play in Winnipeg makes sense. Because he succeeds at making the Yellowjackets Winnipeg's team. Bigger than the Bombers. The Jets don't make the radar. The morning radio vibe, *JCTX's Beefs and Bouquets*, is inundated with calls. The city is vying for the illustrious Glacier Cup, and everyone is excited to the bones.

The press makes polite introductions. Even the querulous older sports hacks admit they are a little more adept at covering the little man in the pocket. A geyser of wisecracks, wagers and predictions becomes the currency for good manners. In other words, Beau and Myles are non-existent. A warped plastic press pass: Angel's crummy excuse for not shaking hands is the sacred buffet.

"It's all about putting up Ws. I think I've proven I can find wins. The politics over who's starting—its's not an issue anymore. I've earned the spot. Just watch today's game. I like Vancouver. But I'm not here to make friends. In fact, I think Pacific College finally understands we're a tough football club. In other words, Gas Town is looking for a jerry can."

A widely respected coach. The quarterback. The communication channels broaden, and acquaintances from each other's corner demystify. The burden to understand each other staggers off the field. All the malicious rumor mill exhaust follows. They are unhitching the hate; bits scatter in different directions, and virtue stands solid to be met by their slowest companions.

The stadium; the scrappy sky with orange, red, and cumulus clouds; the spectacle: it just makes the friendship run deeper.

"Six points is not impossible to overcome." Angel hears the words of Coach Walsh, and senses a quick come back is in the works.

Karla sits up in bed, goes over to the curtains and imitates Vivien Leigh from *Gone with the Wind*. I'm rather jealous: all I can come up with is a scene from Burning Man.

We spend the night in the hot tub drinking beer, and later go gambling in the little motel casino. We dance to Judas Priest, Kiss, and *way* too much Van Halen.

Karla pauses for a moment before saying what is on her mind.

"So, why would you come here to write about a dead guy who may or may not have been a football star?" Karla gently splashes some water at me.

"Oh, that's easy. It's a rite of passage for guys in their early thirties, to enter foreign lands and swoop up all the good-looking girls."

"No, for real?"

"Because, like it or not, I believe Angel could have been bigger than apple pie."

Karla is too busy to chat. A group of Eastern European tourists arrive, keen on seeing the vast Canadian prairie.

I nervously check my watch. Berni Winters, the sports director at the Keystone College, wears a full-length buffalo coat. He turns at me and says he has to take his daughter to hockey practice. Besides, Coach Walsh is the one to talk to.

Coach Walsh has trouble warming up to me. I can tell he has a lot on his mind, and I'm the last person he wants to see. I order drinks and try and act disinterested, but that proves to be the wrong decision. We watch sports highlights on the bar's flatscreen TV and, funnily enough, that works to break the ice. Indeed, that is the only thing that could have broken the ice. He begins to speak like a sports broadcaster—and suddenly the dreamland of sports disappears, and he focusses on Angel's career.

"I don't mind saying he was no different than someone like a Tom Brady, Wayne Gretzky, or even a Michael Jordan."

Coach Walsh remortgages his house during their winning streak. He searches out jobs in the NCAA. For a Treherne guy, that's pretty special.

Suddenly it dawns on me—it doesn't sound right. The Beau and Myles factor. The trailer park in the rear-view mirror factor. The perfect football story does not exist.

Angel wears a Keystone College tracksuit, knapsack, and headphones. He listens to Big Daddy Kane. A big Air Canada logo covers the walls. At the turn, a big redhead, with red lips and polished teeth, sings: "Here's the quarterback!" Angel gives a fist pump. No sooner, the other attendant—a gentleman with an 18-inch neck, a tie knot in the middle of his chest and slops of black dye in his thick moustache and eyebrows— continues the chorus: "Here's the quarterback! Here's the quarterback!"

"Go, baby! Go, baby!" cheered the plane.

Angel fist-pumps all the way back to his seat.

The Yellowjackets are in Saskatoon to play the Harvest Kings. The long-lost cousin of the West Virginia type, the oversized Saskatchewan fans (known to eat hot dogs twice a week for supper) hold their girlfriends in their arms. They give the evil eye to Winnipeg players.

The final score tells the whole story: Yellowjackets: 60; Harvest Kings: 3.

Angel sees Thomas, who moves to Saskatoon to play for the Roseville Spartans and now plays second fiddle for the Harvest Kings. He stands on the sidelines, ambivalent about Angel's performance. He's already plotting a career back in Humboldt.

"What's the matter with you?"

"I've never smoked anyone that bad before." Angel's head is lowered. He has trouble adjusting to their success.

Even a little blip on the scoreboard, showing the Wild Rose College in the lead, can't shake the pandemonium.

"Let's go. Option 11, right side, with a look down the middle."

"Why don't we put it in the end zone?"

"We'll talk about it in the next huddle."

Javi Jones holds the most sacks so far this season. He has two so far tonight. He drives through the upper body and drops 290 pounds on Angel's knee, which ripples through the ankle.

The most inveterate sports fan puts their hand over their mouth. Most remain in shock. Some continue to eat their hot dog, and use a tweaky voice to ask who is going to play backup?

The filthy contradiction: Angel is not an invincible football player. He sheds his uniform. The Yellowjackets' colors are interfering with his personal safety. He eyeballs a blue sky, and tears begin to swell.

The day you go out camping, and you try to take the serpentine metal spike out of the ground. You're searching for the axe. You slam the dense ground, harder and harder, and finally the tent collapses. Players ease out of Angel's line of vision; others feel a little flattery by all the attention. It is a last wind for most. Tears flow on the battle-scarred faces; men cover their noses. Most have never met the young man.

"What's the score?" Angel has trouble saying the words.

"They came back and won: 22–21."

The dream of football glory vanishes. He's gutted by the injury, by the surroundings, and the evil this place can inflict on you. He fails to connect with the nurse or with Dr. Moore, who jogs down the hallway to meet an old friend. Angel feels the rejection and scoffs at the rebuffs—but they are louder now, and the words suddenly have sting

He'll scream the ball up the field for the rest of his life. How do you eschew the strengths of the game now? How do you best the traditions, the lack of warning? And be honored here— celebrated, cheered as an immortal! Angel knows the cries: they are lies, and fake, and false hopes. There's no one breaking bread, offering tobacco, exchanging salutations. This is a time of great clarity, to say enough is *enough and I'm walking away:* slowly, perhaps, but walking away nonetheless.

I'm not in the habit of going out to an airport without either picking someone up or waving at jet fuel, but Cameron suggests we try it out. A little bit of prairie hospitality, I suppose. He has two pieces of lemon meringue pie. I order a Greek salad, which comes with a hard-boiled egg on top.

He has all sorts of blame issues: he feels disowned, like he lost a huge investment. He's lost his boy. Next, he is brooding over what could have been. He plays with the lid on his coffee cup.

He tells me, in a companionable way, that his family is originally from Vermont. His grandparents move to the barren Canadian prairie to take advantage of the free land offer.

I have an irrational sense of American patriotism. It comes out at the oddest times. I point at the ceiling and recall FDR's first inaugural address: "The only thing we have to fear is fear itself." Cameron doesn't like my answer.

"I love my country. But Vermont is pretty cool. Then again, it's very dangerous there now, compared to here."

"Be proud of your ancestor's choices. To be honest, at the turn of the nineteenth century it was a none-too-pretty time in the United States. Slavery was alive and well. Your family made the right choice to leave."

A respirator is in the corner. A shelf with perforated labels—mouth, nose, and ear kits are neatly wrapped in moss-green towel-like paper, secured with hospital tape, becomes a feast for the eyes.

"It's a high trauma injury. But we don't see and deformation, just misshapen.

Angel tries to compute what Dr. Moore is saying. But there is a *lot* of big words, and he knows he is still experiencing trauma. He pushes himself up on the hospital bed. The news sounds mostly positive—but, instead of offering a reaction, he slowly looks towards the window and awaits what comes next.

"We're concerned about the blood vessels around the injury. You know, the membranes around the bone. Of course, because the bone penetrated the skin, there's some concern about contamination around the wound."

Dr. Moore returns, and speaks to a nurse over his shoulder as he inspects Angel's ankle more carefully.

"Rest," said Dr. Moore.

"Yeah, rest—and then I'll feel better. I'll rehabilitate

myself. I'll come back and play again. I've heard that song before."

"You are not in any danger. Your body will heal. It will perform miracles for you," smiled Dr. Moore.

Each day is a grind to find meaning. Ultimately, the shame becomes overbearing. One doesn't slam the door on a throng of screaming fans and walk away, as easy as it may look and sound.

It feels a little more 'prairie' as you enter the Keystone College campus. The long drive up Bison Drive feels a little naked, save for Prairie Field, which builds in momentum on the left side. The vast stretch of green, and an indescribable sensation begins to mount inside you. An existential confrontation happens, and you discard any definitions; you've found the most intense place on earth.

A university with modest reputation but full auditorium. An energized professor speaks, and suddenly ideas brim over the side. A ceiling light buzzes. The overhead projector performs like it is brand new.

"From afar the painting looks very logical, geometrical, rectangular stripes of uniform width in pursuit of...yes."

"What is the title?" asked Angel.

"The Marriage of Squalor and Reason."

The professor turns on the classroom lights, and the picture disappears from the screen.

I sit on the hard sofa in the hotel lobby; Leah comes over and sits down beside me. She smiles, and wants to play: "Who's going to blink first?" I am anxious to get the interview on track.

She's begun ordering devotions from mega-churches

in New Mexico, Texas and Nevada. I ask Leah: "Why Christianity?" She pauses a moment. She purses her lips. She shows me a quivering smile.

"You really are cruel, even though you've written for *The New York Times*," said Leah.

I de-stress in the hot tub. I hold a Budweiser and juggle a cold facecloth. I try and understand Leah's transformation. It takes a nosedive from her previous life, into depths of Christianity, to even talk about Angel.

I chug my flat beer. I hold the cold metal against my outer arm and reflect on her choices. It makes perfect sense: her indignation is merely a little bit of tit-for-tat at cuddling up to someone who is touted to be a big star.

Her commitment to her family is impressive. She constantly changes her looks, and meals are made to perfection. They attend church, and the experience swoons and turns into a game to make next Sunday even more interesting. The posture of the minister, the way the choir sounds, the dress code of the congregation, right down to the conflict of interest at someone snoring in the back row.

She succeeds at her ability to chide, rib, and make others feel sore for her by continuously stirring the coals of the past. Yet, she easily bemoans anyone else for making similar references. She'll always say: "That is irrelevant".

The wind pushes snow against the wide front doors, making it difficult to open the front entrance. A self-possessed security guard comes over but takes no notice: he's engaged in some misanthropic routine. Angel lights a cigarette. The door resembles a worm farm more than anything else. A scream of students enters the warm building. Angel acts clumsy, hiding his cigarette. He wants to stay, but his mind is already in hot pursuit of other dreams.

His eyes are heavy and pensive.

"I don't think this is for me." Angel looks for a moment at the Professor, who has sat down beside him.

"It's metallic black paint. He is trying to find what he called emotional ambiguity. He felt a little resentful about the romanticism of the abstract expressionists. Not sure if he succeeded or not."

But this can be an exciting time for a boisterous young man. He is finding strengths in the classroom, obtaining all A's last semester. He is keen about an academic career. Madilyn and Cameron, on the other hand, are struggling why they have to put all of Angel's gear up for sale on eBay.

Angel sits on the leather couch and watches *Jeopardy*. Serialized science-fiction movies replace football. A cola and a red straw rest on the shiny glass table. His parents are distracted by the expensive TV. He uses an old Yellowjackets jersey as a pillow. He tosses the football back and forth; he zips a fast ball into the corner of the end zone. No—instead, he flicks the ball and spins it on his index finger, and motions he is open for a Steph Curry trey.

"Why are you taking her side?" Angel screams, raising his hands in the air.

"If she thinks you're going out, then you owe her an explanation."

"Not really."

"Enough." Cameron holds up his hand, desperate to halt the conversation.

"Leah has been your girlfriend since you were 16 and she deserves an explanation."

"Then I'll call her." Angel places his hands on his head; he feels misunderstood.

"I just want you to be a man about it."

Angel slumps his bullet-head to his chest, with dejection and relief that he no longer has to discuss Leah—ever again.

The Christmas holidays represent a respite from all the drama. The house is dotted with Christmas decorations.

Madilyn wears a denim dress and black turtleneck sweater, with a lime green necklace. She wears her makeup thick, and pitter-patters joyously around the house. She fills candy dishes with jube-jubes and multi-colored hard candy. She pours glasses of sherry. She reinvents herself well enough, where everyone joins in on the fun. It's invigorating but, with the absence of football, it all feels a little contrived. Or if there *are* a few laughs about their new life, everyone suddenly feels on edge. There's also the sense of humility about their new life, and there's something always imperfect about new humility. You never feel like you're soaring. But Angel, and his mom and dad, still don't know what to call any of it.

Cameron watches Dan Marino cover a mid-season matchup between the New Orleans Saints and the New England Patriots. Cameron is left huffing and puffing, undecided whether to watch the game or help in the kitchen.

He can go downstairs, and revisit some of his latest pleasing woodworking projects. Cameron's tiny kiosk at The Craft Fair has built up a pretty impressive business, selling Seahawks, Dolphins, and Giants key holders. Madilyn asks he put aside his woodworking for everyone's mental health. But he remains obstinate and continues to plug away at them whenever he can.

Cameron puts on his slow-dance eyes and watches Madilyn prepare roast beef, pan-fries and string beans. The setting is uncomfortable and awkward, but the mistrust is placed squarely on Angel. He has become a burden.

A long snow has dumped on Winnipeg. Angel, eager to prove his fitness, goes outside and begins to shovel. Each stab at the ground is a close call, believing he will cause more harm than good. But the front and back are finally done. He swells with accomplishment.

Cameron greets Angel at the backdoor. They exchange funny faces: the perpetual grimace about the 'incident' plays heavy in their rapport.

"I've never been to NYC." Angel scratches his chin.

"Your uncle lives there."

The last time Angel met his uncle was a very long time ago. However, the memory is etched on his mind because his dad and uncle get into a fight in the back yard and knock over the BBQ. The fight ends before it begins, and soon after they are acting goofy getting each other beers. Or light each other's cigarette. Later, while Angel's parents are dancing to a popular Genesis song, his uncle comes over and gives Angel a heart-to-heart talk. The purpose of their talk is to reassure Angel that he was not really fighting with his dad. Angel has no right to say he experienced trauma. Angel scoffs at his uncle's overprotective nature and tells him to relax.

"I was just making sure you weren't upset."

The walls are covered with prairie landscape portraits,

and Angel points to an open spot near the front door.

"Why don't we have any of his paintings?"

Madilyn looks quickly at Cameron, and then enters the hallway.

"Because your father refuses to call him and ask him for a painting."

The years of shared commitment comes to an end. Angel is in a state of panic for what comes next. Madilyn and Cameron are missing the point of the importance of his life: what comes after football. Cameron does not renew the lease at The Craft Fair. Madilyn joins a writing group and a knitting group. Cameron goes to Walmart to buy some hardware to mount one of the 4Ks in the master bedroom, where he stops at the island of clearance books.

Angel reaches for the book on the kitchen counter. He leafs through a few empty pages and puts it back down.

"What's up?"

"I thought you could make millions writing books. Maybe start writing a journal and you'll figure things out."

This is by no measure passing-off the responsibilities of parenthood. This is a decision handed down by John Huey, the father of pragmatism, telling Angel to make the right decisions. Winnipeg, with its crushing nostalgia and burbling melancholy, is not helping. Time to find new goals and actualize one's potential.

Originally, the injury means being cut off from games. Certainly, no more calls from recruits and a free lunch with some members of the press. Recently, the change makes breathing difficult for Cameron and Madilyn.

Hunter scratches his way through high school in

Regina. On weekends he creates 40-feet paintings, and launches them off different grain elevators.

After a few years working at dead-end jobs in Regina, the celebrated art magazine *ArtZine* sends up a reporter with little clout to cover Hunter's trial. A group of soybean farmers claim his artwork has a negative impact on crop prices. Strangely, Hunter, becomes very confessional in the interview and claims he tries to come out in high school, but Regina society will not have it. Years later, now a huge success in New York City, Hunter is once more the subject of controversy. A group of gay rights activists say Hunter used *ArtZine* to promote his art career. Hunter writes the editor: *You never met Alice.*

MANHATTAN

I once lived here when I studied journalism at Columbia University. I am in the heart of Sugar Hill. A hop, skip and a jump from the Apollo Theatre and Central Park. This is Black America. Leaving my front door, it is either hot, cold, drizzling, or time to wear a scarf.

I live in a derelict building on 126th Street and Broadway. On weekends, I go downtown to SoHo. The streets are cobblestone; the buildings are medium height with an inordinate amount of iron work. A lot of used furniture shops, art galleries, antiquarian book shops, hidden Michelin restaurants. Abstract painters still have studios here. De Niro just walked across the street.

Angel eyes the scratched plastic screen between the front and back seat of the yellow taxi. He feels a little claustrophobic. The speed of the taxi is dizzying. They cross the Triborough Bridge. A twilight sky breaks behind the Manhattan skyline. The scandalous East River is full of boats. The thump of the bridge. A bill-fold full of cash. The driver feels Angel's urgency: let's start to live.

He exits the taxi and looks up Mulberry Street. He admires the simplicity of the design. The cobblestone street, and the big patches of tar. The continuous blare of honking. The buildings, which seem to lighten as you look up, painted in a light grey. They're fashioned with a complex web of iron fire escapes. Some are covered in burgundy rubber tree, jade, and various species of spider plants. Or Chinese bamboo mats, accompanied by Ray-Ban intellectuals who sit outside like Spiderman and breathe heavy thoughts.

There is an uncourtly group of garbage men at the corner. They wear fluorescent overalls, and one worker has a St. John's sticker on her helmet. They tend to switch from an easy smile to a grimace rather quickly. They have long necks that point towards their next garbage pickup. A group of twenty-something techies crosses the street, scampering over the bumpy cobblestones.

Hunter wears a gold suit. He holds red roses. His mouth has bits of dry blood at the corners from the silver grill he had fitted earlier in the day. He owns the forbidding street. He represents the New York art world. Very few critics dislike his work.

The differences between his dad and uncle are quite extreme. Angel spends some time trying to figure out how his uncle could possibly have come from Regina. He rejects the comparison and admits his uncle has a flair for survival, a bit more so than the rest of the family. But the good fortune of meeting his uncle on a Manhattan street is bigger than the family connection. He sheds their history and instead smiles politely, but also hides that he is a little shocked about his uncle's success.

"You make sure to always tip. Evil will impose itself upon you if you don't tip. People take revenge on someone who doesn't tip properly here."

But Angel's euphoria of living in Manhattan outweighs any family advice. He reaches out to shake his uncle's hand, which is quickly swiped away, and fussy hugs follow.

Countless families come to NYC to start a new life, and Angel does the same. He is anxious to act like a New Yorker. It will be perfect—the irreverent countenance—and face any challenges with simple instincts how to survive.

He unpacks his belongings in a roomy corner bedroom that Hunter builds before he arrives. He looks down at the street below and tracks his eyes to a desk of drawers. He opens the plastic Footlocker bag and removes the journal his dad has given him.

Journal entry:

I recall hanging out in downtown Winnipeg and going into this famous dollar store on Portage Avenue. There would be row upon row of plastic flowers, or else, a stockpile of bars of soap. And conditioners: hundreds of hues different pastel shades. Who buys this stuff? I meet Sally. She would own bags of this stuff, and someone helps her at the door with the bags.

"She's wild and sexy with me. She's in that zone. But this is New York City. You know I could have taught at Keystone College or in Saskatchewan at Living Skies College, but no, I chose to come here. I sold my soul. It was 1988. I managed to turn that trip into a mildly successful career." Hunter thumps his chest as he looks out the wall of windows overlooking SoHo.

"Okay." Angel looks in disbelief in either direction.

"But I'm not scum, so don't look at me like that."

The loft is about two thousand squared feet and has different living areas. A glass sliding door with a small wooden terrace overlooks Greene Street. Angel pushes the glass sliding door open, believing the conversation is over.

I wear an old pair of khakis and a NY Rangers sweatshirt. I'll sometimes throw on a Pebble Beach cap. I march up Broadway, believing I am going to be the next Jack Kerouac. Every encounter, every experience, while I am sober, is an attempt to reward my memories, to someday share my life in the pages of Penguin, Knopf Doubleday, or Vintage.

All the driftwood you meet doing menial jobs starts to pile up. Angel's group (Carlos, Mohammad, Giovanni and Ivan) are no closer to Jack Kerouac, Allen Ginsberg, Gregory Corso, or William Burroughs, than I am writing an Oprah book-of the-month club pick.

Mohammad Laghari comes from a good family in Queens. He is provided the finest opportunities anyone can ask for: a progressive Muslim upbringing, wherein his family works tirelessly to dispel negative stereotypes. But the defenses cost him dearly. No, Mohammad is as patriotic as one gets in America. But the role to dispel the myth about being Muslim hardens him, and he is bored by the message. No longer does he have the verve to help others understand his heritage. He wants a nice girlfriend. Some pocket money.

Carlos Garcia is an illegal alien from Southern Mexico. He walks across the Nuevo Progreso, Tamaulipas, border when he is 17 and has been working a 13-hour shift ever since. On most days he is so exhausted by the number of hours worked he cannot tell you if he lives in Mexico or the USA.

Maria turns their teeny-weeny apartment into a meeting ground for all those coming to Manhattan for the first time. He speaks to his family for an hour each night. But the impermanence and risk of deportation affects Carlos. He disbelieves in a normal life. His entertainment consists of counting whatever money he has in his pocket.

Giovanni Simmons is from Harlem. His dad is a chef, and his mom teaches opera at The Juilliard School. He is expected to apply his natural gifts and achieve his potential. Or something that resembles his potential. But tedious little fights get the better of the small family. His parents overplay the tough love card, and tough love loses a lot of kids in America. Giovanni is too caught up in the game to try and improve things with his parents.

Upon entering high school Ivan is obsessed with his *Foreign Affairs* subscription. Downtown is an occasional visit to Wall Street to meet his dad for roast beef and Alaskan king crab lunches, with a tall Roy Rogers and crushed ice. The East Village or the West Village: they exist above ground as you take the subway to Wall Street.

Later, he mopes around his parents' immense Upper East Side apartment, discussing screenwriters like Paddy Chayefsky and William Goldman. His mother calls for an intervention. The psychiatrist says we're here because you need to stop talking like Steven Spielberg is your cousin.

Hunter asks me to meet him on Houston Street and Greene Street in SoHo. He pulls over in a punctilious black van, full of paintings and some sculpture. We cross the famous Brooklyn Bridge and eventually arrive at our destination: a well-preserved pink, red orange brownstone in Brooklyn Heights. He opens the back of the van and, without any explanation, proceeds to throw the paintings across the yard.

He angrily comes over to me and scoops my tee collar into his fist. He has no intention of going on *20/20* and speaking to the well-mannered Keith Morrison "...so let's get it right!" We talk a few solemn words about Angel's death, when he stops me from speaking:

"What do you think of Sally?"

He makes me feel like an addict, at a point of addiction panic.

This is how I describe my state of mind while I think about Hunter: I'm at a party on the Upper East Side, hosted by a famous businessman. From the other side of the room, a man stares admiringly at my legs for what feels like an eternity. I get up and go over to the man and ask him if he would like to smoke a joint on the balcony with me.

"Let's say I walk in after painting for 16 hours and you're eating quiche Lorraine together. I'll ask you how your day went. I'll explain some of my musings while I paint. I'll politely ask you which window you would like to jump out of."

"Okay, I get it," I answer, unsure if I'd used the right words.

"I'm kidding. Sally is yours, dude."

We drive back to Manhattan in tongue-tied silence. He manages the music, the air conditioner, or he takes a call. But he refuses to talk. He makes it known that we've become close.

Ivan calls me and says he wants to meet. Before I can answer, he is ensnarled in a stream of consciousness, and I have no choice but to listen. He finishes his monologue by saying, "The Strand is very large."

They break off and check out every nook and cranny. Two pretzels later they sputter out and, before they come over and talk to me, they blaze a thick joint and pass it around.

We walk a few blocks and go to the honored Astor Place, where we find a quiet bench between Lafayette and Fourth Avenue. It's late, and a dance erupts between buskers and traffic. The busy working crowds are replaced by hipsters and grungy characters, who are comfortable at speaking to no one in particular, remaining fascinated as they spew into the night sky. A lot of religious drivel, it appears.

Mohammad whispers "Privacy" and starts to repeat it, louder and louder. They meet me because they think I am a celebrity. They know how to push the right buttons and get a reaction out of me about some athletes I've met in the past. They like to manipulate me for the sake of manipulation.

Angel debates accepting a job at a used clothing store in the West Village. He settles on a waiter job at Believe, a fashionable restaurant that specializes in Mexican and Japanese cuisine in Greenpoint, Brooklyn.

Angel decides to explore Manhattan. He takes the Subway uptown and gets off at 76th Street. He walks along Broadway and imagines new storefronts to replace the retail space available signs or filling his cart from Free Value and Beyond. He reaches 74th Street. He finds a little bar.

It is post-World War II style bar with black and white tile floor, long wooden bar, mirror shelves and an impressive choice of single and double malt whiskies.

It has a sinister atmosphere. The bar is full of mostly men. Most of these Joes are smarting from their treatment towards women and assume the edge they've been delegated to non-domestic duties.

"What's your story, Mac?" The bartender straightens

out the service area, replenishing the fruits and spices.

"I'm an adventurer."

"Wisecracks can find the door."

Angel snatches a peanut and tosses it high up into the air.

"Your peanuts are way too salty."

"That's so you can order a second beer."

The scrawny bartender comes over to Angel and rests his hairless arm on the bar. For a split second he offers Angel the feeling that he's worth a million dollars.

"This place could be your stomping ground."

"I can't decide if I'm getting drunk to stop the noise from outside, or from listening to you?" Angel takes a handful of peanuts and focusses on the hockey game on the TV.

"Go back to Staten Island." The bartender points at the door.

"I'm from Manitoba."

"Oh yeah, well sorry for you, pal, because I have no idea where that is."

The Subway works. Strange how the dirty platform and the exhaust-stained ceramic tile walls, or the black-encrusted cement tunnel, becomes an acceptable place to rest one's eyes, thoughts, and purpose. The jostle of the train; the doors opening and closing; a sense of purpose ignites, and you are better for your next adventure.

Angel speaks a few unimpressive words to the haunted peanuts man but doesn't have the compunction to say too much more. He spins and looks up at the skyscraper. It's Trump Tower, and then there is Central Park. Or 57th Street. All these places belong inside an F. Scott Fitzgerald novel inside the blithe River Crossing library.

He catches a Rangers game at MSG. Then stumbles through the multi-purpose arena, where the ghosts of Marciano and Joe Louis remain, thirteen Rolling Stones concerts later, and where Hulk Hogan reigned as World Wrestling Champion.

The Helvetica-font Bedford Avenue Station sign welcomes you to Brooklyn. He discovers Park Slope, an artsy section of Brooklyn, a few stops from Manhattan on the iconic L train. He tries a slice of Brooklyn pizza. Just like the movies: greasy, and the perfect match of pep and 'za. Nice flop, a classy bite! A bookshop with a popular display window: a full list of Paul Auster titles, and first edition copies of *The Boys of Summer* by the amiable Roger Kahn. Angel goes to the back and orders a cappuccino, which includes a nice dome of foam and rust-colored sprinkles of cinnamon. He returns to the front and sits down on a lonely bench.

The easy smile is suspicious. The body language is violent and impetuous; courteous explanations are put on life support. This generic gentleman has a sense of entitlement. He appears to be staging an attack on Angel. All this guile is hard to imposture.

"You're in the shot."

"What?"

"Dude, we're shooting a picture. Our cameraman is on the roof, and we need this shot."

Angel stands up and inspects the storefront across the street, and finally spots the group of filmmakers, dressed in black from head-to-toe, on the roof.

He approaches the group of protestors. He admits he doesn't offer enough curb appeal. He's going to get a mouthful.

"Why don't you take those animal carcasses on your feet, that strip of animal membrane around your waist and die."

"Do you need some money?"

The protester looks Angel up and down but cannot deny Angel's honesty. She cracks a wry smile before turning belligerent.

"You sound so stupid and ignorant. You make me sick."

Hunter and I sit inside a restaurant in Chinatown. The walls are bare; the tables are covered in thick plastic. We drink green tea, which he says he adores.

"Did Angel paint?" I push the menu towards the edge of the table.

"No! I already knew he could paint," replied Hunter.

We go to Central Park, where Hunter stops to light a fat joint. The earthy smoke leaves a skunky trail. Two young men in tan leather jackets approach us. One of them pulls out a silver-looking Western gun and demands our wallets. Hunter continues to smoke his joint. Next, Hunter runs at both of the men, swinging his arms widely, hoping to hit anything in his path. The gun goes off several times. Then it falls, hidden in the dirty snow. The two men, realizing how much they need the gun, search frantically through the snow. I begin to hyperventilate, thinking we are going to die.

My encounters with Hunter are hard to understand. He is an important artist. He is the reason I decided to write about Angel. Recall, I could have taken the gig at *The New York Times* and penned some edgy piece on some unsolved murders in Brooklyn. But New Yorkers get a jab of murder every day. He won't let go of my arm. It's the only way I can put it. There's some sympathy for the man who goes along with it. Our meetings are easy for him. I was at the mercy of a silly game of tag that literally keeps me awake at night at how close I was to dying.

I was a little worked up:

"Let's get some guns and go after the bastards!"

"Just breathe easy and decompress."

My greatest fear is this is going to be traumatic incident that stays with me for the rest of my life. I can't stop trembling. Hunter turns our encounters into expensive affairs. I am not proving myself as a writer. He needs me to prove that I am a man—but in ways that are totally unknown to me.

*

Angel, Hunter, and Sally relax inside the loft after a pleasant meal together. It has been four months or so and they feel like old friends. But Sally doesn't like the tranquility. She steps up her conversation with most everyone she encounters. Angel will be no exception. Their conversations cover topics like Islam, acupuncture, breast augmentation (which Angel seems to have lots of good ideas about) and tattoos. Sally likes to reminisce about her family. Her father once dated Lee Harvey Oswald's second cousin. Angel asks whether he was a man or a woman.

"He's mad talented." Sally applies lipstick and then swings her hand for her glass of wine.

"I know," said Angel.

"This is not your typical Art Students League success

story. I could have gone to Paris."

Sally stands up. She steps up onto the sectional and sounds off like she is overcome with Angel spreading lies about Hunter.

"...she's got more talent than me. But we're also fighting misogyny *all* the time."

"We're really tied up into gender equality. And not at all in search of a gender equality, that very safe place that New York intellectuals love so much. We prefer to say that women are better than men. Are you okay, Angel?"

"He's my brother's son. He knows what equality looks like. You have no idea how intense and hot and important these topics are here."

Hunter's words trigger a whitewash of silence. But Angel is amiss at being discussed in the third person, especially by this uncle, with whom he had never developed a relationship. Suddenly, Angel asks if perhaps his dad has a much closer relationship to his uncle than he is aware of. The uncertainty allows Angel to reflect more critically about his family, and what they might be saying about him. Suddenly he is overcome with warmth and comfort at being in in their company. He dismisses the bit of attention, and admits this is how all families act.

"You're figuring stuff out. Sally just told you a feminist has a hard time sometimes."

"Isn't that an oxymoron?"

"Oh, I like him." Sally stands up and circles around the spacious loft.

Romeo Hernandez is 6 feet 6 and has a hollow-cheeked, pock-marked face. His hair is crinkly, with a part that starts at the back. He wears a *Sopranos*-style, barbershop shirt. Black pants. He is unfriendly. Intimidating. He looks in the mirror when he's upset to calm his nerves.

He builds himself up by overreaching at garage sales in the five boroughs and sends oversized care packages back to Honduras, as many as one hundred times a year. First helping his family and extended family. Then helping schools and local charities. He begins to make modest political donations. Soon he's swapping Levi's for pushing heroin.

He is elegant helping his family. Next, he is sopping wet in the back of a Cadillac at Newark airport and deflecting insults from a crime boss, who warns Romeo he will shit down his throat if he doesn't stop worrying about the interior leather.

"Just calm down. And you won't die."

Romeo spends a little bit of time in prison for tax fraud. The ones interested in working with him are on a similar path. He has helped elect as many as four presidents "back home." Working in politics is novel and uplifting. The political process is inherently corrupt, but we always need someone with good hygiene in front of a podium.

Angel gets off at the Greenpoint Avenue subway station and walks towards Believe. Inside, a large dining room, on the far wall, the pièce de résistance: a mural of a CN train barreling down a teetering bridge.

Luna wears a running top. She has dark hair and dark complexion, and wears silver eye shadow, which off-sets her natural colors. She uses the tables like an exercise machine.

"What's up?" asked Angel.

"Nothing. My girl is just getting me down."

Carlos straightens the cutlery on some of Angel's

tables. He puts the napkins over the side plates.

"She gets nasty."

Luna overhears Carlos.

"Don't mention my name!"

"*Shhh.*" Angel tries to calm the waters.

"Don't shush me, Angel! He's talking smack."

They appear clumsy as a couple, but they soon find a bar in the East Village. Luna orders cheese bread. They are their normal selves, reaching over the small table to touch each other's face.

He tops up Luna's wine glass. Luna unabashedly talks sports. How reserved Angel becomes. He acts like a librarian returning Luna's books to the stacks. She talks so glowingly about the Heat back court, or else why the Patriots can't lose on Sunday. *Speak up! Open your mouth! Say what you have to say! You have every right in the world to say something!* Angel's eyes brighten at every miss, and dabs a little more polish at each name that Luna swoons over.

They lie in bed and are silent. It's not malicious. They have nothing to say. They each feel unconquerable.

The large open kitchen has an island in the middle, with a Dean and Deluca ceiling and complex floor-tile pattern. The fridge and stove are standard aluminum finish. A strobe light is attached to the ceiling, hidden behind a hanging shelf for pots and pans. On the ceiling: a strobe light with a *Blade Runner* affect.

"I'm surprised you're related to such a big cat," said Luna.

The painting swings slightly on the exposed brick wall, and now Angel lurches over to save the small glass covered painting from crashing on the kitchen floor.

"Your uncle is famous."

"Yeah."

"But you know the male-female imbalance."

"My girl is a lawyer and I'm a waiter. She knows I'm on a leash because I'm illegal. We deal with a lot of stress."

Angel listens to Luna's stories, but they are not making ground. Nor does Angel appear like the perfect catch. Their time is numbered.

A group of newly hired wait staff stand outside and smoke, deep in knotty conversations on a plethora of subject matters. Angel slips past, avoiding saying hello.

The restaurant is preparing for a staff meeting. Carlos wears a leather jacket, white tee, and ripped jeans. Angel quickly gets dressed and enters the dining room.

"Canadiano," hollered Carlos.

Instinctively, Angel goes over to the wall of tables. They push the tables together; the gathering of lamps resembles a bonfire. The CN train is at full throttle, jumping tracks, hurling down the flat, barren, empty prairie.

Journal entry:

I'm acting daft, standing here, arranging these tables, attending this meeting. There are no Yellowjackets on the wall. There are some issues with understanding each other, certainly pressure to make rent. Some others would like to climb a little higher in their job. Certainly nothing like a football game.

Angel indulges his mistake at just being here.

Inside Romeo's office an old metal desk with drawers

on each side is pushed up against the wall. It remains a curiosity as to how it got into the small space. Or it remains an after-dinner conversation, somewhere in the Bronx. A day worker holds a forest-green bottle. Finally, he brings the red grape to his mouth, quenching whatever stress remains. Newspaper clippings of Karl Marx, Che Guevara, and the newly elected president of Venezuela adorn the walls.

I go to the Bronx. I stand in front of a cage of well-mannered monkeys and eat pink popcorn. Someone taps me on my shoulder. I turn and find a thick Hispanic man with a gentle smile and overlapping front teeth. He hands me a black envelope.

This is Weinstein at a small after-party in Sundance, where *Vanity Fair, Hollywood Reporter,* and *The LA Times* are mingling, and two very young actresses are getting zippy on Oxi. Or at a board meeting, where Donald Trump gets stung by an unexpected zinger, which makes him look like a peach croissant.

Romeo puts a muzzle order on anyone to ever speak to me. He bullies a judge and insists on an injunction. Next, he threatens to sue the newspapers. We smoke some Nevada weed; I explain this is not about him, and he caves.

The morph of Believe: the focus is about learning as much about merlot and Beaujolais and pinot noir as quickly as possible. It's always just a veneer, which a glowering Romeo will later destroy.

"We're like the UN. Look around and you'll see all different races and ethnicities from every corner of the world. It's no accident. I'm not holding you hostage, if that's what you mean? Leave. Am I criminal for getting you papers? For arranging places for you to stay? Am I a criminal? For giving you money every night? I don't think so."

Romeo counts bills into small piles of ones, fives, tens and twenties.

"Know your role," Romeo counts out money in his hand.

"Yeah." Angel nods, feeling out of place.

"That's two hundred and eighty dollars. No tax." Romeo hands Angel a wad of bills.

Angel puts the money in his back pocket without counting it.

"I don't pay taxes because you are my labor," said Romeo.

"I get it."

"Did you ever hear about the twenty-six million Russians who died in World War II? I think I owe those knuckle heads something."

"I'm not into politics. I'm just trying to get some pocket cash, you know, while I'm here, knocking around the Big Apple."

Romeo overtakes people with an inflated sense of himself, and a defiance for the rest of the world. Others are petulant until they become part of his entourage.

"I want you to attend a meeting, to understand more clearly what I just said," said Romeo.

There's no discussion in the matter. Once more, Angel feels like he is a cog in the wheel. He has no say in the matter. He must follow Romeo's orders, because that is what Romeo wants. It is part of the job mandate. To Angel's shame, even Romeo's sinister intentions are lost in the request, as Romeo holds an unfair balance of power in their relationship. Moreover, Angel comes to the appraisal that his own presence is forcing Romeo to say the things he is saying. What is paranoia? Or would Romeo have acted on these demands with anyone? Angel recognizes the ugly side of narcissism, and quickly dismisses their conversation as ordinary and follows Romeo's orders.

"Carlos will show you the ropes," noted Romeo.

A little competition grows between Carlos and Angel. First, they come from outside the United States. Carlos is from Mexico and Angel comes from Canada. They both file taxes in the USA using the names of two different adult men—close in age, and whom they've never met. That sense of being an illegal somehow comforts each other. They are each equally indifferent about what that means, politically, and share some laughs at how recalcitrant their predicament causes them to act. The major difference is Angel looks like he grew up in Brooklyn, and Carlos, well, he has to wear an FBI windbreaker to stop any curious looks.

Carlos makes a joke upon learning that Angel plays quarterback in college. Romeo stops Angel and takes the bread basket.

"What's wrong, man? I thought you were my *Monday Night Football?*" said Romeo.

Angel is not sure how to react. He decides to play it like he no longer cares about his football past.

"You know Luna attended Connecticut, but she couldn't afford the tuition?"

"She never told me that." Angel looks at the tables awaiting to be cleared.

"That's why she's my girlfriend. Hurry up, clean those

tables, Montana."

Any slips (you want to open a place of your own someday) is strictly forbidden. Members of Romeo's crew are prancing around with their pants around their ankles. They are licked victims in a game of male prostitution. Prison is one of the simpler pleasures of life. You eat in a spiffy restaurant on the Upper East Side, and the bill arrives. You decide to get up and not talk to anyone. You go over to the tightly packed coat check and make conversation. Arrangements are made behind your back to cover the sirloin and side of asparagus.

He holds so many gifts at arousing their trust: *We'll host an after-hours party, shower you with gold and silver bling, women, even celebrities. And make you look godly, with so many little hustles on the side.*

Carlos is a little rattled. He takes Angel aside and stares deep into his hazel eyes. Carlos understands Angel, his apprehension about living outside of Canada. He grabs the back of Angel's head.

"You've got to help me out, man. I need you." Carlos looks around the room. His eyes are dilating.

"I've got you."

Romeo organizes a night of cultural activities Uptown. It includes several Latino musicians, numerous poets. The guest of honour is a journalist from Honduras.

This is the world of Washington Heights, the other side of the world from Brooklyn. A passport costs one hundred dollars beside the *New York Post* stack. This is where huge populations from mostly Central and South America arrive to make it big in the world. The pressures are tremendous (drugs, street violence, gangs) and it ends up being a much harder life than back home. But courage is found, and on some nights the American dream feels stronger here than most other places.

Hip-hop clears the smoke. You finally understand: corporate America doesn't want any part of this place: rows of uncertified goods, no-name candy, artificial soda, doughy chips, and stretchy acid-wash jeans are pinned to the chipped wall beside a flickering sign with the latest lotto numbers.

"Yo."

"I want you all to meet the crew," said Carlos.

The group of young men huddle together, but inevitably (unwise) make each other feel a little uncomfortable. Yet they have shifty eyes, enough to make it work.

At one time they all work at Believe.

"I worked as a waiter. Later I was a driver. I went out on my own. But I'll work for the G-man whenever he needs me."

"You delivered shit."

"I delivered beer."

"Same deal."

"We're just getting our history straight."

"And now we're all connected for life."

"Word." The group nods approvingly.

Mohammad begins to push away from the group. "Actually, I don't think this dude really cares."

"Of course I do," said Angel.

"I'm just messing with you."

"We are not supposed to be instruments for the government. You have to make a choice about how you want to survive. You either feed your family, or else you're looking over your shoulder. Y'all have a moral duty to fight and go and get justice."

"I come from such a different place. But this is a really wild."

"Soon you'll get the hype."

Young guns with a hard story. An endless stream of melodrama that could dampen the night chills of a Broadway playwright. They stand under a yellow awning, with thick red lettering: Hector's Fruit. Wobbly tables hold waxy boxes with holes on the side, with wild California farm names, full of assorted fruit. A few buckets of dank and fowl flowers block the entrance into the cheap-o store. A leaky hose, the nozzle spraying, blocks the entrance. The energetic and poised group easily overstep any obstacles or impediments and enter with anxious grace.

Black boots. Red lipstick. Thick woolen sweaters, with black tights, and a black leather Chanel purse over their shoulder, and invariably push a baby cart in the other. Dudes in Yankees garb, Starter jackets, with brush cuts. And just plain—to-the-curb, no-scratch, pinchin' squat—poor people. Where someone finds any hope, motivation in their life is a miracle. They believe in social justice!

A young man wears a thick puffy jacket comes over to Mohammad, opens his jacket, and jabs a short blade into Mohammad's side. Instead of continuing his attack, he steps over Mohammad and rushes out of the scene, acting like he's just topped-up his tough-man street cred.

"He got me! Get him, Angel!" Mohammad checks where he has been injured.

"He's gone." Angel looks down the street. He holds the side of Mohammad's head.

"Why didn't you stick him?"

"Angel doesn't need no rap," said Carlos.

"Yeah."

"I saw his face," nodded Angel, as he looks up the street.

"This happens because we look weak. Others think they can walk all over us. He wanted to notch a strike on his street cred," said Mohammad.

"Word."

The clouds turn dark. Angel's heart begins to race. He is not in his element. A brazen self-awareness emerges: *and why shouldn't I strut through life like this?* His face transforms into parts unfamiliar.

"And when Angel yielded his knife, he fled. I could see his eyes. He knew, you feel me? He knew we were just as hungry as him, to build our street cred."

"Listen Mohammad, I'm sorry. This was not supposed to be like this."

"It's all good."

At Believe, they are turning customers away. The cooks and wait staff are overworked. Since Believe has a big front window, with an airy, almost terrace feel, customers might wear a fur coat and scarf during a meal. Romeo is on, stoned and a little shifty because of a disagreement with the dishwasher. The kitchen is not any sense breezy or creative; the darting eyes search for any kitchen faux pas. A violinist enters the bistro. He plays *Requiem* by Mozart.

"I've got to go. My friends need me," said Carlos.

Romeo ignores the capable business he has built from the ground up. Even to see him scheme, flip, and ignore the restaurant responsibilities and make sure his crew is okay, shows a hard personal philosophy. He obsesses over conflict and is in shatters at resolution. His politics are accidental to the young men he trains and forces to attend radical political meetings. And none of them are run-of-the-mill followers anyway. They seek out free lessons on social movements.

These are Champagne Commies, and hold a Philly cheesesteak. Romeo uses Karl Marx the same way a bookie might muscle a client. It has nothing to do with his love for the proletariat—he is collecting kneecaps.

But through his work he becomes connected. It does not make life any easier. He works a 15-hour day. But admittedly, there is no second-level expertise.

He comes up from downstairs. Believe turns silent. He is an unknown, brash heavyweight coming from the dressing room to the ring at Madison Square Garden. All eyes are swollen at his approach. First the kitchen, the dining room, the street, and the violinist decides to leave.

"Mohammad is in trouble. We got to go and help him," said Carlos.

"Call me, if you need anything," replied Romeo.

There is a sense of unflagging commitment, dressed in bravado and complicity. They're engineering excuses—how to break out, so they're not culpable. They comfort each other, living on the edge.

It is the same taxi that brings Angel in from Kennedy. The dispossessed driver recalls Angel's urgency to live. Angel peers outside at the stick-up men, at the cops, at a few hookers (who make us doubt the meaning of a flower shop), a card shop, an anniversary. Let's just score, score, score.

*

They meet at the mouth of the 148th Street subway station. Ivan wears a tight-fitting black jeans and striped shirt. Mohammad has his beard trimmed at some b-boy hair saloon that prefers DJs for clientele. Giovanni wears a no-name tracksuit, which cost one thousand dollars. He is accessorized with diamond bling, gold chains, with a ribbed tank undershirt. Carlos and Angel are in jeans and hoodies and MLB caps and have glossy eyes.

The gargoyles stretch a mean stare over New York City tonight. An elderly man walks his poodle. Two short, elderly women with paisley plastic hair covers drag empty shopping carts, manœuvring laterally as passengers get off the bus. A postal worker, clad in messenger bag, worn-out Velcro, hustles up the street. Two Black women exit the hair salon, with new braids.

"Don't think that's the dude."

Carlos removes a black pistol and cocks it, waving it slowly to reveal the underside, and both sides, evenly.

"We've got to make it right after what they've done to me."

"Let's do this."

"You're not going to kill someone for this."

Mohammad is flummoxed by the lack of respect. He lifts his shirt and shows the long scar near his heart.

Caesar wears a low-cut black shirt, and black baggy jeans. He wears a black bandana, and gold on each wrist. Mila Morales wears tight jeans, which tapers over a small leather boot. A black blouse, accessorized with high-gloss plastic bracelets, and creates a nice bridge over a navy-blue BMW hood, Connecticut plates.

As soon as Caesar comes out of the restaurant, Mohammad, Carlos, Ivan and Giovanni separate him away from Mila and drag him down the renowned street.

Angel doesn't know what's going on. He tags along at a safe distance. The curtains lift on Broadway. At once, the executive cars appear to have stretched slightly, press on the gas a little harder. Even the crowds who spill out of the restaurant morph into the exotic. Mohammad shows his piece to a few passersby. The tone is set. The streets don't much mind a little murder tonight.

"Yo, man, let me go."

"What do you got to say?"

"What are you talking about?"

Mohammad sticks Caesar at the waist with a 10-inch blade.

"Do it."

Angel goes over to Caesar and pushes up against him, so they eventually look into each other's eyes. Angel's crew begins to laugh, believing Angel is going to do something extreme.

"Come on. He said he didn't."

"I go to Pratt."

"Let him go."

Angel takes Caesar by the lapels and separates him from the others. Caesar grabs Mila and they run up the street.

They sit in the sombre back seat of the taxi. They rest their eyes easy on each other. The taxi stops; no, it screeches. Angel looks for ahead into dreamy destinations. Carlos can afford a chuckle at the luxurious address. Angel breaks though the noisy metal gate and climbs the freaky metal stairs.

The crew from Believe mark their territory. Angel doesn't know what that means exactly. Except it is time to leave ... the clatter, the smoking drugs, messing around with Luna. Or the indignity of working 'under the table'. Mohammad's money problems. Ivan: the silent discomfort about his crew. Or witness a mind like Giovanni: a remarkable mindfulness only to pass over life's better side for drinks and a little atmosphere. The only closeness he wants to New York City is when a postcard falls on the front door mat.

New York puts him in an irregular space. He finds a quiet café, an open floor in a Midtown skyscraper, which houses the homeless. And such a juxtaposition: fifty floors and counting, and trendy aluminum table and chairs, and polished pine wagons that sell exclusive high-end coffee delicacies. The man by the window nods approvingly. By chance he is wearing three parkas. He holds his teeth in one hand and two raisin scones in the other. And free *New York Daily News, New York Post,* and the *New York Times*. A copper sits alone and eats a sandwich in wax paper.

The curvature is two multi-level ramps, where the Pacific College fans waddle from the parking lot to plastic seats. They hold binoculars, hot dogs or nachos, and plastic cups of beer.

Two people see each other. She flaunts gold teeth. They smile and laugh. He is auditioning for *Midnight Cowboy*. But never mind the funny interplay. He is hailing a cab and going to the nearest cheap motel. Next, calling his mom: "I'm getting married!" Or they make love in the back seat of a taxi, or on a new park bench, painted in the famous New York forest green. They attend the Met Gala and waltz cheek to cheek for six hours. They awaken and they are married and ... she breaks for the door: "I must go and take a morning-after pill, but we'll talk."

Chanel shoes, tartan mini skirt, and a Levi's jean jacket buttoned up to her neck. A Prada bag. She dreams about big turns behind a fluorescent speedboat. She might be in her sixties, but tells her boyfriend she's 34—why not?

He recalls a documentary starring Rauschenberg, standing at the top of a clunky ladder, because that is where Bob wants to do the interview. He talks about his work. But speaking on any other subject, he sounds off. It's similar to when a fastball big-league pitcher begins to talk about God; the next time you see him pitch it all seems a little off. Don't ask an abstract expressionist painter about your horoscope.

Hunter dedicates an enormous amount of time and energy at nurturing Angel's interest in art. Why not attend a painter colony? Angel acknowledges he needs to make a final decision.

Sally calls me and asks me to meet them downtown, at Union Square: and you'll see Hunter in action. Hunter signs one hundred black and white postcards.

Angel comes home with a painting under his arm. He takes it into his room to hang. Hunter appears in the doorway and offers to help. The two bond like never before.

"After Hunter leaves, I was planning to seduce him," said Sally.

"Excuse me, Sally?" Hunter shakes his head in disbelief.

"He says, 'I guess I should have asked my uncle if this was okay?'"

Sally transitions from calm as a cucumber to the

Waterford crystal smashing on the exposed brick wall back at the loft.

"I'm just telling you the truth!"

Freezing winds sweep up the great avenues. Each intersection is a mass of snowbanks: cars spinning, honking, and NYers with thick scarves and tuques manoeuvre through the sloppy ground, and somehow collectively deny it ever gets cold in NYC.

The Metropolitan Museum of Art: the famous grey cement staircase and wavy banners promoting the latest show looks like a Christo installation. A sea of yellow taxis stretches up Fifth Avenue. A little further uptown resides the Guggenheim. A few blocks downtown, the Ritz: the most exquisite hotel found in the new world. Any richer, Yanks risk calling it tacky.

I find the row of artists, just like Sally describes. I meet Norman Addison, an abstract expressionist painter. He is not quite abstract enough to open downtown, but in front of the Met he looks like a movie star. He remembers Angel like he is his only son.

Norman is a transplant from the 1950s. He wears baggy denim overalls with a cantaloupe-colored waffle shirt underneath. Tan work boots. The mandatory thick beatnik black-framed glasses.

"What do you want to give me?" asked Norman, who begins to place a new painting on display.

"Just browsing."

Angel peers at the other artists and notices the dissimilar styles of art.

"I'll give it to you for free, as long as you can crack it." Angel looks contemplatively at his newly acquired work. "It looks expensive."

"Yeah...."

"And you used a knife. I'd say it's abstract." Angel holds the painting, tilting it slightly to get a better angle.

"Abstract expressionism."

Norman removes the painting from the table and begins to wrap it in brown paper. Angel continues to act indifferent, for he does not want to show how genuinely excited he feels at receiving the free gift. He recalls his time in Winnipeg studying art history, and suddenly he feels like an old hand at understanding art. Norman, however, can tell that Angel is not your typical customer, which is why he tries to help out the young man. Meanwhile, Angel is being taught a life lesson about the value of art, of how quickly it perishes for those who put together a few bits to make it happen.

"Remember, next time it will cost you one million dollars."

His appreciation for art explodes. But he anchors himself into a trance and stares disquietingly up the open street. He searches for deeper structures across at the park: the trees (the American elms, Black Tupelo, and London Plane); the psychedelic reflections on a passing black limousine. The trust and decorum of a capitalist culture: an East Indian family stroll along the street in synch with the zeitgeist of our times.

One expensive dream after another. Even the piles of debris in the South Bronx tonight, in every corner of the State, the fallen structures represent expanse and growth. Let's extend the spirited subway line once more.

Carlos leaves his Greenpoint basement apartment (no windows) by 5 a.m. each day, so he can prepare hungry-man breakfasts at Mexico: eggs (any choice), pan-fries,

Canadian bacon, homemade black beans, and— mostly— various varieties of rye bread.

Inside Mexico, a series of artsy black and white photographs adorn the walls, of men, mostly, standing beside a donkey. For some, a sample of late nineteenth century racist portraiture. For others, an example of Kodak technology.

The staff wear tees with a red chili on the chest and bullfighting hats. A series of taco garlands hang from the ceiling. You can order a mariachi band (they need one-hour's notice).

Carlos says goodbye to Maria. She works at a temp agency for two different credit card companies. Angel holds the door for Maria, who pushes a baby stroller with Carlos Junior smiling and playing with his baby giraffe.

Angel gawks at the menu board, scratching his chin.

"I've almost had enough of Mohammad and the others. Man, I could use a ball game," said Carlos.

"Yeah, let's plan something for later," Angel scans the menu board.

Carlos takes a notice of the painting that Angel is carrying.

"Word. What is that?"

Angel shows Carlos the painting he was given at The Met.

"Oh, just a painting I picked up."

The two friends speak some solemn words about the painting. Suddenly, they feel embarrassed, for they have connected through art. Carlos dismisses the epiphany; indeed, he cracks some joke to the cook in Spanish.

Angel and Ivan meet on West Broadway in the West Village. Ivan describes himself as a good Jewish kid from the Upper East Side. Romeo's crew will fall off eventually. Meanwhile, he tugs on a joint, and mumbles under his breath; smoke rises from his mouth and nostrils. Suddenly, he stops in his tracks and begins to mimic rolling a movie camera. He buys a Sony camera from some street hustler and discovers a fossilized rock inside. He palms my back. And says he's going to show me how to kill someone today.

"My uncle might be able to help you out."

They run up the street. He'll end up going to NYU, or sneak into Brooklyn Law, and have a second home in the Hamptons. His mother repeats this dream to several of her closest friends.

Giovanni has adoring eyes and takes comfort at knowing his mom is somewhere within its magnificent structure. Juilliard. She understands his predicament. He has been stoned for three days and finally tries to get things straight.

"I usually sit in this bar and drink cranberry and vodka for a while. You see, across the street my mother is teaching kids to sing on stages all around the world."

"That sounds noble." Angel takes a sip of his beer.

"Until I can't feel my legs. An ambulance once had to pump my stomach in this very chair."

"Can I say something?"

Giovanni straightens the coaster under his drink; however, he doesn't have the strength to bring the drink to his lips.

"She never once bad-mouthed me. I messed up. I kind of lost my career like you."

His blue-collar manner goes against the grain. He cannot keep his end of the bargain. Living in the same building as James Baldwin didn't help him worth shit.

The streets are a little darker, but the brownstones are no less impressive. The thick traffic, and store fronts with modernist window displays attract fussy customers. According to *Time Out New York*, the East Village is a destination for a good meal out. It's full of exciting little shops (clothing, art, books, music) that causes passersby to take notice. Later, with the added purchases, they are armed to dictate fashion trends to their closest friends.

Mohammad studies English at Hunter College, when he starts to work at Believe. He gets hooked on crank and some other illicit drugs, which Romeo is more than happy to supply. Pretty soon Mohammad forgets about completing a PhD on William Faulkner and offers to drive Romeo around whenever he needs some muscle.

A man enters the bar. He wears a tartan pant, Doc Martens and thick leather jacket with a Nazi symbol on the back. He removes his jacket, revealing a thick neck and stupid arm and neck tattoos (The Kool-Aid character and a KitKat on a surfboard.)

To put on a thick leather jacket with a Nazi symbol on the back is huge. It is not only a poor fashion choice, but an invitation for a universal decorum of insults. Smirking, coughs, sneers—and even bursts of laughter—pelt you from every direction. The choice of which jacket to wear becomes a delicious dilemma: the world hates you and you put on a dirty jacket anyway.

Mohammad tends the bar, while Angel smirks at the man a few stools away who only barely breathes, and whose life is under our control: he has lost all expertise in the most basic dignities of staying alive.

"What's the matter, are you prejudiced against Neo-

Nazis?"

"Yeah, a lot," said Mohammad.

The man with the Nazi jacket moves down the bar and sips on his rye. But he shoulders a hard side glance, knowing full well that Mohammad and Angel are mocking his existence.

"Get this: I ask this guy: 'Why do you wear a jacket with a Nazi symbol on the back?' He says: 'It's warm.'"

"Yeah?!" chuckled Angel.

"You know, the Velvet Underground went out of business a long time ago."

The noise inside the loft is like standing on the subway platform. The city accepts the extremes as a function of its brilliance. The people Angel has met so far resemble the other side of a two-way mirror.

The city makes you stronger, and you're ordering a double rye with your scrambled eggs, and toast with raspberry jam.

They meet at a bar in the East Village. A metal garage door covers the front entrance. Mohammad slams his forearm against the door. Suddenly the clamorous door rises, and you're facing a huge crowd. A rap battle engrosses the crowd. Ivan buys a bottle of whisky. Giovanni chimes in with one of his own. Next, they are on the roof, dancing. Maria shows up with two of her friends. Mohammad's girl reminds the crowd why Queens has such a hot reputation. Ax, the West Coast rapper, joins the party. His crew makes no bones about the East/West Coast war. Angel talks with his friends but finishes too many beers and too many hits off joints, with unfamiliar rooftop vistas. At one point, Mohammad tells

Ivan he intends to split the rapper's head open. He calls off threats after Ivan has an anxiety attack.

Angel wears a tracksuit, and fluorescent hunting tuque. He is nervous. He lights a cigarette. His knees knock; he taps his toe like a thick cigar into the snow beneath his large, athletic frame.

An endless crowd shuffles through the New World—it's unsustainable. The electricity is hidden behind buildings, in the clouds, approaching the subway station. And as you feast, or the need to find energy to survive, you're in fact exasperating the situation. The lolling around, looking, droopy, creates missed chances to smile at a stranger. And Angel chooses to see his friends again and again.

There is a song by Mumford & Sons that mentions it. There is the film *The Basketball Diaries*, which Leah always moans over. And, of course, the movie *Kids* the film by Larry Clark. His professor tells the class as soon as he arrives in Manhattan, he stops at his hotel, makes a Manhattan, and then ventures out to Tompkins Square Park, to say *I finally found you*. It is found at the corner of Avenue A and Seventh Avenue. The leafless trees are set at irregular angles. It gives the impression of a thick forest. And little lamp posts illuminate randomly, triggering a disorienting sensation.

The park is covered in a blanket of snow.

His mobile phone rings. He looks at the name on his iPhone. For the first time since he's been in NYC, he looks forward to his dad's affected voice.

"Hi, dad."

"How are you, son?" asked Cameron.

"I'm Okay. I'm actually witness to something right now." Angel looks anxiously towards the other end of the park, where he sees Ivan, Giovanni and Mohammad approaching an unsuspecting young Black man.

The leaves swirl. A dog walker, a spoiled boxer, chooses to avoid the park today.

"How's my crazy brother?" Angel almost drops the phone. He stares for a moment longer towards the group inside the park.

"I think I see some friends messing with someone right now."

"Just never mind. Just keep your nose clean and stay away."

Suddenly, Carlos appears, and he doesn't notice Angel is on the phone. Carlos can hear Mohammad and the others in the park, he motions for Angel to follow.

"What's going on?" asked Carlos.

"You don't mind if I just don't join you guys?"

"Oh, I see them." Carlos lightly jogs towards the group in the park.

Time passes, and an inexplicable swarm of action takes place around his friends. But Angel watches the swirl of ferruginous, oatmeal, and amber leaves, the benches. High above he notices the lectures inside roomy lofts that encircle the park. Despite the opulent window touches, there is a strong avoidance of the outside world here.

Suddenly, Angel is hit from behind. Cameron's jawbone is broken. The ear-splitting sirens in the background awaken both of them simultaneously. Or the man across the street, who pulls the leash on a black Labrador retriever and decides to laugh like a crazy man.

The sirens grow louder. Neither Cameron nor Angel wants to be the first to speak. They're embarrassed by the silence. Cameron gloves the mouthpiece of the cheap cordless phone and speaks loudly at Madilyn.

There is a kerfuffle. A morose and now contrite man is being pushed around like a pinball in a high score game. Mohammad, Ivan, Giovanni, and Carlos widen the elliptical circle. The man in the middle drops all defenses. His pleads are one last stand. The others are deaf. Death and darkness have already packed it in. Indeed, they are putting on mascara for the performance now.

They check out each other and nod angrily. Giovanni removes a Glock and first puts it at the young man's shaved head. Mohammad tilts the young man's face to the sky. Ivan removes his Mercedes Benz tuque. They scream. The young man pleads for his life.

Angel continues to stare. The only wittiness. But there are others, hidden, many like him in the blustery winds of tonight's murder, who all do the same silent walk and dance. "Look it's stupid, shy and depressed ... I believe brilliant just walked by."

Obviously, Cameron loves his son. And wants the best for him. Besides, Angel didn't fire the pistol, and so, according to Cameron, why should he give him up?

At last Angel begins to move: a shamble, now padding the cold ground. But no longer as a young man with hopes and praises for anything he has accomplished so far. Alas, he belongs to a longish line of aggressors over men and women of color. He cannot keep up with even the most crooked man of faith.

Consequently, Cameron and Madilyn are even further from understanding their enigmatic son's life. When they could hold him in their arms once more.

Angel hears his dad on the other end of the line scream

to leave the precarious area. He looks down at the body. The Black face. The twitching eyes, and the lantern-jaw, bloody bucktooth. A soft improvised whistle turns his teeth pink.

Carlos screams. The scattering of the park, a gusty wind, the scattering of leaves and snow. The weight of just dumping oneself to the ground.

"We do this. Let's go!"

I am in the hotel parking lot in Winnipeg, and I approach Cameron's SUV, a white Ford Sport. I shut the driver side door. Cameron unrolls the window, and swings his elbow over the side: "Why would Angel tell me something different?" I wear a long-sleeved denim shirt. He reaches over and straightens my collar. He's caught in a lie, and murder doesn't catch his fancy.

Angel mentions the conversation to Hunter: paranoia and unwillingness to help a Black man.

I owe this kid something. But that is as religious I'll get about it. And murder happens here. We are a product of a lot of murder and seeing it is nothing new.

As I walk through the powerful Washington Square Park, I see their defiance. The aching resentment is really just fussing over them. The internal battles, as some wimpy smile appears. You come to your senses: you've never held them accountable. How convenient it must be to know their guilt.

The foursome scoff at my story. Carlos begins to inquire where I am staying. "I'm in a nice little room, overlooking a big park. Do you know which park I'm referring to, Carlos?" I keep repeating.

I'm inside The Craft Fair, and Madilyn holds my reedy arm. Cameron talks to Nate, who has an impressive Elvis collection. They appear to be talking about me rather loudly. Madilyn takes my arm and offers numerous rebuffs to my questions about Tompkins Square Park.

"I prefer we ignore that little episode in New York City." Or else: "I don't like trying to remember that nasty bit which you seem keen on always bringing up. Am I not your guest? So?" And inevitably she states: "Please can we turn our focus on the right other stuff."

Madilyn takes on the aura of knowing about the incident better than anyone. She is alone with Angel. She pushes him away from the violence. A mother does not put her son in such circumstances. Tony's discovery is nothing more than a typical American obsessed with violence.

Carlos runs over to Angel and grabs his arm to join the others and leave in the waiting SUV.

"Let's go." Carlos tugs at Angel's arm to leave the park.

Several minutes have passed. Angel shuts his phone. He stumbles out of the park. He later finds Mohammad and the others smoking a blunt a few blocks away from the park. Angel approaches, but they are too high and incredulous to pay any attention to him.

"Get over yourself. Who *we* are."

"Why do we have to go? When we should be helping him."

Mohammad pulls the trigger. He is a murderer. He sees Angel's suspicions and wears the discomfort like a superfluous piece of bling. Besides this punk-ass was pushing crack, and he knows the game, and why not clip his ass?

A tall red head returns into the restaurant. It is not Sally nor one of Sally's friends. She laughs and gently turns to say hi to me. Hunter wears a vintage Muhammad Ali robe. He has a string of LED lights braided through his beard and hair. It's one thing to get a tip to write a story, but quite another to sit across from a stately man who snorts coke while talking strangely about lentil soup. Invariably, you start to administer your own cocktails of drugs to make him better.

Hunter rents a space on West Broadway to launch his latest series of works. It has a glass front entrance. There is a table full of postcards, books, and even some umbrellas and T-shirts. They are also selling a Damien Hirst knock-off: a squirrel skull covered in jelly beans.

Angel stands across the street and watches the crowd. There's only a trace of respectability: little groups, lots of male couples, and a friend who tags along and smokes inconspicuously. Or the beautiful Black woman, with her head half shaved, and one long coiled dread that looks like a snake. The pedestrian traffic—holding heavy and light and medium plastic bags—shoulder a blank smile at some of Hunter's work. A kind of visual rape, it happens all the time in New York City.

Angel feels the Crown Royal. He feels the rich and focus-like reality TV has nothing on him. He lives and breathes his new life. The crowd tempers a slight shoulder push towards the front entrance. An ornate iron spiral staircase leads you up to the second floor, where an acid jazz band plays.

"Angel, you made it!" said Hunter, taking a sip of wine.

"I wouldn't miss it."

Sally has several youngish men, twenty-somethings, crowded around her. So, when she takes a sip of wine there is an explosion of eye contact, innuendo, and backstabbing.

"Your aunt."

"Oh." Angel nods, thinking it's time to leave.

"Just relax—I watch her have sex with other men sometimes."

"I don't like hearing that."

"Just like your old man: you've never taken an interest in my life."

Angel remains mute. He is neither self-conscious nor ashamed, for his uncle is saying things that make no sense to him anymore. His uncle's manner puts him in a difficult bind. Angel veers his head around the room, and quickly realizes that was the wrong move: everyone attending the opening tries to sneak a glimpse of Hunter. Angel drops his head, nods politely, and slowly walks away.

Angel walks over to the bar and grabs a beer.

"Okay. Uncle, why is it okay that you watch your wife have sex with other men?"

"Mostly younger guys. In their twenties. You see I almost lost her, and now we're back together. Just be on the lookout."

Angel recognizes they are on different paths. The matching DNA fails to brighten the atmosphere.

"Can I buy a painting for my dad?"

"Go ' head, pick something out. The ones with the red stickers are sold. Choose anything you like between thirty and fifty thousand." Without the slightest hesitation, Hunter pushes Angel through the crowd and points at some paintings.

"Fifty thousand?"

They sit on the L train; Luna swings her curvy legs over Angel's legs. He puts his hands between her thighs. She holds the back of Angel's neck and lightly squeezes. As the L accelerates, she stares at their reflection in the darkened window.

It is a heavy-metal bar on Mercer Street, loaded with industrial design: open ceiling, vents braiding in all different directions. Metal reliefs cascade down the walls, with purple smoky colors streaming through an assortment of devil motifs.

"Sounds to me like you're a murderer," said Luna.

"Excuse me?"

"Ivan and Mohammad wouldn't have touched that kid if you had gone over."

"You can't say that." Angel tosses the of ArtNews onto the coffee table.

"But that's what you think? Why should I forgive you for something like that?" Luna slides her hand through her hair.

"Murder happens all the time in New York City."

"You think we're actors down here? You could have saved him!?" Luna holds Angel's shoulders from behind, and then kisses him on the cheek.

She sits on the bed, covered in crisp sheets, and giggles as she admires her fluorescent nail polish.

Later, on an uneventful winter day, Angel tidies his room. He decides to chat with Sally in the loft area. Sally is from Albuquerque. At first, she pursues becoming a filmmaker. She likes Hal Hartley movies. But that all changes at University of Texas. She is transfixed with Richard Linklater. She tells Angel the story of addressing her class after a screening of *Dazed and Confused*. She doesn't understand why they keep watching a movie starring Lance Armstrong, when he was kicked out of bike racing.

"Lance Armstrong didn't star in *Dazed and Confused*."

"Don't you get the irony of disagreeing with me?" Angel feels no compulsion to disagree. The imagery reverts to the chatty classroom:

"Yes, it seemed absurd. The movie was way too Lance Armstrong for me."

She disappears for several hours. Angel remains on the black tweed sectional and watches back-to-back episodes of *This Old House*. Finally, Sally returns, showers, and sits back down. She politely asks Angel what he misses most about football.

He sits at the back of Believe and cleans the minimalist, heavy, stainless-steel cutlery. Frank Tuddy, an undercover FBI agent, comes over to Angel and begins to ask him prying questions. Nothing seems out of the ordinary. Erving, a mid-career FBI agent, sits by the window, drinks a Shirley Temple through a straw with two hands and looks like a knot of nerves.

Romeo reaches out to no fewer than four informants in the past week looking for a little bit of action. He starts to talk like he's a big man. The Feds are making moves. On paper, Romeo is as clean as they get: he owns a restaurant that is rumored to earn its first Michelin star this year. Except he is a suspect in no fewer in four rather messy murders.

Angel looks through a hardcover picture book of de Kooning pictures. Hunter nods and raises his glass to the ceiling and points the #1 sign into the thick cigar smoke-filled air.

"I got accepted into College London."

"You're just going to leave this place?"

"Yeah."

"Besides, Luna is more interested in being my life coach than a girlfriend. I just need to leave."

Weeks turn into months. Angel is becoming restless. Hunter gives Angel cash to carry around. If he sees something that strikes him, he owns it soon after. He agrees to foot the bill for London: the apartment, food and clothing.

Large ferns act as a camouflage in front of the lights, splashing multi-color designs all over the spacious loft. The bartender stands inconspicuously behind the table, ready to make any variety of cocktail. An impressive selection of assorted wines from California are arranged on the table. A small jazz trio play.

"This is my crew." Angel introduces Ivan, Giovanni, Mohammad and Carlos to everyone.

"Looks like a bunch of degenerates." Hunter reaches for a cigarette.

Sally rushes over to Hunter and puts a joint in his hand, and helps him bring it up to his mouth.

"He's been looking at a canvas all day."

"I'm sorry," said Hunter, refusing to be genuinely apologetic.

"I get the artist temperament," said Carlos.

"Of course, you do. You're beautiful. You understand a lot of things better than most of us."

"Yo, have you been drinking?" asked Giovanni.

Hunter swings his fist in the air, and now chuckles as he takes another hit off his joint.

"Step back, or I'll ruin your world."

"My father practises law in New Jersey. My mother is an event planner," retorted Mohammad.

"Next."

Hunter is drunk. Angel's friends are not the type to accept anything other than a nice compliment about their parents' background. But Hunter acts indignant that everyone answers with solemn sincerity. Angel looks at his uncle with desperate eyes, in hope they can find a polite way to end the conversation. But that is not going to happen. Instead, Hunter acts defensively and begins to take easy shots at the guests. The chance to turn the party into a *The Talk of the Town* event is out of the question.

"Y'all are going to do what with your lives?" Hunter grabs a bottle of champagne from the table and swings his arms wildly while he speaks.

A waiter comes over and offers Carlos a glass of champagne.

"I want to open my own place someday."

Angel recognizes the unfair treatment towards his friends. Hunter's anger is even more pronounced when he speaks to the waiter: he rolls his eyes as he grabs the champagne bottle. He smacks his hands together, imitating that he is holding a clapboard whenever the waiter speaks to any of Angel's friends. Angel's friends are not inclined to act as they would in their own home. They have become targets for Hunter's erratic behaviour. Angel calms down at the thought that everyone can leave at their discretion. Certainly, Hunter will not stop anyone from leaving—or will he?

"We'll figure something out." Angel stands up and tries to bring the discussion to a close.

"If you have a passion, nothing can stop you."

124

Ivan and Giovanni walk along the balcony and enter Hunter's bedroom. They stand in front of one of Hunter's paintings. Ivan starts to remove the painting from the wall.

"Yo! Take this! This is the beginning of our career. He can't sit here and talk like that."

Everything about Believe is legitimate. Romeo merely shows he is concerned about the beef Wellington and nothing else. But the Feds have to start somewhere. Angel seems like a logical choice to divulge on a complex web of politics, drugs, and dirty street crime.

Angel is part of the political mudslide and, if he digs in any further, he might end up in prison. A junior agent with the FBI, Frank Bello, more closely resembles Snowden than someone trying to climb the ranks in Virginia. Frank sees Angel as a possible informant, and he makes his move.

The night begins innocently enough over a few beers. Three or four sex-on-the-beach shots put both men on the floor. They end up at a Staten Island strip bar, which has an inordinate number of Eastern European dancers— purple metallic lipstick is all the rage.

They stand outside the strip bar. They sense the possibility of getting whacked. And then, rather mysteriously, a courteous countenance comes over both men. The mob rules these streets: they have not become friends, and going their separate ways seems the easy next step.

The rest of the crew get a similar interview to Angel. But, so far, no witnesses have come forward, and there is no CCTV footage. The crew refers to Angel in the third person. A possible realtor in Nebraska, but nowhere near the scene of a crime in New York City.

Angel is college-bound. Yes, he's an illegal alien—but Hunter can vouch for him.

A swarm of movers take over the loft. They exhibit chilling expertise, collecting rental wine glasses and some light stands, and breaking down the bar. Hunter agrees to purchase all of the ferns. Upon seeing the empty wall, Hunter drops the fern. The medium-priced Chinese porcelain bowl shatters; a plume of soil covers the hard wooden floor.

"*Untitled* above bed is missing," Hunter points at the floor as he speaks.

"How could you accuse me of something like that?" Angel puts on his jacket.

"Because your friends are insecure. And capable of a lot worse."

"I could say that about any number of people I see in New York." Angel pronounces his words slowly.

Hunter dismisses Angel immediately, and his naïveté assumes a sense of self-corruption.

"How much are we looking at?"

"Five to ten." Hunter grabs another painting from the wall and tosses it across the loft.

The dollar amount was not outrageous. Indeed, Angel had imagined much greater sums for a painting—but it was the *volume* of paintings that his uncle creates that was cause for concern. Angel recalls visiting his uncle's studio and seeing hundreds of these kinds of paintings neatly stacked on the floor, or against the wall. There were many others, much larger ones, hanging on the wall, or even larger ones still attached to the ceiling on a pulley system. The combined total of all the paintings would easily reach one million dollars. His uncle could blow up at any moment and say the painting was worth much more.

"Your uncle is not some pick-up artist sitting in front of the Met, you know."

It feels like all the walls have fallen in around him. He is safe, but now his crew is on the hook. And Angel, despite not being witness to the theft, feels doubts are surfacing like a speeding car.

"I've called the cops. Otherwise, I might end up killing someone ... and yours will be the first neck I squeeze."

It looks like Blondie's Lower East Side studio apartment, and Lou Reed is strung out examining the electric box for three days. Meanwhile, Andy Warhol begins the painstaking process of stencilling a Michelangelo painting on the ceiling. Mick Jagger and Keith Richards are in the kitchen, fighting over some silly bit about the Champions League.

Hunter achieves the status of New York artist and then some. The most banal and boring parts of his studio have explosive meaning. Suddenly, Angel feels like he is imposing. Putting the groceries on the counter feels unnatural and lacks conviction.

Sally wears a houndstooth miniskirt, purple leather boots, and black bra, and an oversized Van Halen pendant. Hunter gets hot flashes thinking about Angel's crew. It is his own version of *I Shot Andy Warhol*. Hunter remains frozen until the police finally arrive. The police walk in, and someone says they thought they saw a woman without a shirt on.

"We've talked to Ivan and Mohammad; quite frankly, they don't seem like the type."

"Oh."

"I'm not saying they're incapable of doing stupid. But

they are not *that* stupid."

Upon seeing me, his face turns white; aqua-blue eyes; and crusty hair slicked back. He is tortured at the memory of the stolen art. Suddenly he becomes defensive about, well, the fact I am 6 feet 6. And could I change into shorts and a muscle shirt?

This is a political act of sorts. Hunter assumes the reign of power and makes quick and easy decisions at who's in and who's out. A hamstring injury would not wash here. He's had other pieces stolen. Once from a low-attended vernissage in Palm Springs. Another time from his Greene Street studio. He is astonished to later find the stolen work in an online auction, where it is described as a work by Frank Stella.

I feel responsible for his safety. He slams the kitchen cabinet—and how dare I turn the tables on Angel.

"Just worry about the lad. I'd have those dorks stuffed with hay and sold at a Tiffany's auction in an hour if I was really worried. Just worry about my bloody family why don't you, scribe!"

The duties of an assistant in Hunter's studio are a little different than most other studios. A successful sculptor might have an assistant who kneads earthenware clay, cleans fettling knives, cut-off wires, or potter needles, and certainly helps with firing the pieces. An abstract painter has a paint room to organize. Or, reference innumerable ways how to stretch a canvas. But Hunter's assistants end up doing the laundry, make cauliflower pizza dough, drop acid, and sometimes perform sexual favors. Hunter refuses to work with women. Because he feels deranged at being a man. Many avant-garde feminist art critics are sympathetic about his views, but they remain resolute: Hunter is essentially a misogynist and he deserves a bullet at the side of the head.

He sits over a can of paint. Randy helps him remove the lid. They speak a few words. He is given a large ice cream container full of freshly mixed white paint. He wears a black lab coat. He focusses on the canvas until his fatigued shoulders begin to tremble.

"Quite irresponsible to elect mustard head, don't you think?"

He has me down for the count; whatever I say, he will unwittingly unleash a healthy amount of personal wealth—and it amounts to a lot. Suddenly, an unnoticed painting by the window (or Randy, the scatterbrained, muffled assistant in Levi's and a green crocodile shirt) is edgy and dangerous. I can rock a few shoulders, but the trap is set. The game is up.

Hunter stands at the entrance of Believe. He acts defensively, finally disarming and putting the Mexican and Japanese cuisine kitchen staff out of sorts. The importunate sounds coming from the kitchen grow louder.

"I didn't ask him to attend any meetings," said Romeo.

"Oh, no?"

"Besides, he's old enough to make his own decisions."

"Actually, he's rather impressionable." Hunter puts his Yankees cap on backwards.

"We dabbled in a little bit of pro-democracy stuff. Root for the underdog."

"You could have fooled me." Hunter scratches the back of his head.

"You managed to frighten all of my customers away.

But let's open the doors now. I've got to make a living."

Dispossessed, Hunter now owns Believe; Romeo, who has streetwise instincts, can't do anything— save let him let off some pent-up steam. But Hunter is finding personal treasures at every turn: his anger and revenge mount, and sirens clear out.

A small wooden staircase at the side of the room leads to a VIP room, decorated with antique furniture and expensive table dressings.

"What's this?" Hunter senses he is on to something.

"Oh, that's the upstairs dining room."

Hunter can see his own side table, the unmade bed, even his own shadow, as he rushes past the painting going towards his SoHo loft. Here, there is no connection between Romeo and the painting. As Hunter approaches the painting Romeo appears to turn invisible. Hunter looks at the other walls and, for a moment, notices Romeo, who appears upbeat by all the attention towards the painting. But Hunter is overtaken by his anger. He digs deep into his coat pockets. The sense of ownership over the painting is tremendous.

Hunter wanders over to the painting on the wall.

"What, may I ask, is that?"

"Oh, who knows? Adds some color to the room, don't you think?"

"You can't be serious."

"Make me an offer."

"You're a much bigger idiot that you look." Hunter grabs the painting from the wall.

"Don't you like my taste in art? Or are you one of those people who doesn't believe that art can uplift the spirit? Take it. Don't ever come back. Tell your nephew he's not welcome here anymore. Listen, man, I know people!"

I wander through Times Square, absorbing as much as I can. Back and forth, from the neon buildings to the centre of the tourist universe. Again, skyward—at the colossal living and working space of a wealthy universe, then back at the Timberland boots, backpacks, eyewear, and the slight elbow work, oblivious to the market value of this location. It is about being here together that matters.

Hunter sends a limo to pick me up. I am tired eating at the Korean salad bar and so I accept. I am driven to Hunter's private tailor. I ask the driver what that means exactly, given that Hunter only wears a bathrobe: "He got you a Brooks Brothers as a send-off."

The clothing shop is located in the West Village, on the second floor above a tea shop. You enter via a spiralling iron staircase at the side of the building. It takes you upstairs to an impressive pressure-treated wooden balcony, that overlooks the busy street.

Gold carpets; red, hard high-gloss plastic shelves; neatly arranged suits and separates; shirts and ties; and a nice selection of casual and dress shoes.

This is not far from the very strange costume shop found in Stanley Kubrick's *Eyes Wide Shut*. Once the shop closes, all sorts of taboo sexual mediums happen here. I can envisage, for example, fluffing the pocket square of a size 44 navy-blue blazer many dozen times during an eight-hour shift, building some lasting affectations.

The tailor is a small Asian man, with twinkly eyes, and soft wavy hair. He puts me in a blue suit with wide lapels, and any red tie of my choice.

As I sit in the back of the black limousine, I gently hammer the soft red leather seat beside me. Admittedly, I am in a very exciting position creatively. It is like being Annie Leibovitz but— rather than get the pic—I am forced to give someone the Heimlich manoeuvre for three days straight. Or my first trichotomy. Maybe I head a legal defense team on a rather messy rape case. How many men have left their B&B and wonder if they should have put on lipstick for their host? Hunter is responsible for countless men and women dropping out of art school.

The high cost for a few laughs. Or the ecstasy he gets from restraining me. When I'm with Hunter my heart beats louder, my voice sounds different—I speak in a higher octave, and suddenly I'm ready to strike someone with whimsy. Hunter can sit back and take a drag off his cigarette, and contemplate, I suppose.

Randy delivers takeout from Zabar's, the famous Jewish deli on the Upper West Side. Our meal includes knish, caviar, roasted chicken, lox and bagels. I stuff my face and find myself moaning while I eat. I escape the table by pretending I cannot miss a game on TV.

We go to a club in Hell's Kitchen, and he buys me a table dance. I think it is Sally. I get up and politely walk away.

LONDON

2014

Angel reads about David Cameron's promise to deliver a referendum to the British people on the overnight flight. Suddenly the UK's future appears uncertain—a perfect opportunity to enter College London.

Heathrow includes huge walkways, open spaces, mezzanines. A wild variety of people returning home from ten days in places like Panama, Costa Rica, or Jamaica. The feeling of being in the capital of the English-speaking world. To be back on familiar ground, ever so charmed at the recognition of the UK's past appetites. It becomes a matter of organizing the meaning of Empire.

"The Tube?" Angel asks the clerk in the magazine shop.
"Follow the signs, Sir. First time to London?"
"Yes." Angel places a copy of *Details* on the counter.
"Good for you. Johnny Depp and you will have a blast."
"Johnny?"
"The cover, sir."
"That's Robert Pattinson."
"My apologies. And what a fine British actor he is. The lifeblood of London; it will take you in every which way you want to go. God speed!"

The hostel sleeps six people per room. Angel is in deep sleep when he is awoken.

She is tall, has braids, and speaks in a German accent. Angel has a flashback of lying on the football field, his foot hanging on by a thread.

"You're in my bed."

"I don't speak Russian." Angel slowly sits up.

"Go see Gurdeep."

Gurdeep apologizes and gives Angel a new key to an eight-bunk room. He enters the stuffy room and discovers about twenty oversized men, with red and yellow and orange beards, playing poker.

Angel takes a free bunk. A few moments later, a nose and gawkish eyes peer over the side of his bed. The unknown player raises his square, ruddy hand to shake Angel's hand. Someone turns off the lights and everyone falls asleep.

Angel meets a group of Canadians at the International Students Association. Robin is tall and overly bookish for Angel. Robin is shocked at learning that some of his professors are communists. Robin announces that a Prince Albert pancake breakfast at the Esso station might change their mind. No one understands what Robin means. Jeff and Kevin carry a chess board as they scuttle around campus. They scream with embarrassment for hours over a Bobby Fisher interview, at his dirty antisemitism.

The group breaks off and search for apartments in earnest. In between, they acquire a rather disturbing drink habit. Soon, apartments are locked, favorite food joints found, and an affection for the bookish life emerges. Soon they are breaking off important engagements to see each other.

Baptiste has charm and confidence. To meet him might appear a touch intimidating: he holds a little bit of secrecy about his sexuality (which not everyone can carry).

Only to offend Baptiste more lessens the nerves. Baptiste Durand sports round glasses, a red velvet pant, and short leather jacket with a small David Hockney button. His arms are longish, and his movements are slow and deliberate. And he makes any great stage actor fear and tremble at his good looks.

There's no offensive line in front of him, nor any coach on the sidelines, or a girlfriend in the stands. Or even a pair of knuckleheads to quack off questions at the end of a tight game. He takes a long pull off his cigarette. *Ben Hur* and *Porgy and Bess* played here. Suddenly, Baptiste appears. He understands Angel instinctively, and yet Baptiste gorges any sentimentality that Angel might possess.

"What did you think of the lecture?" asked Angel.

"Class, race, ethnicity, and gender are the future." Baptiste puts his foot down.

"What do you mean?" Angel gestures for Baptiste to continue speaking.

"Focus in on the basic concepts, and you've got your College London diamond necklace. We're the workhorse to unearth the key theories behind these concepts. I'm going to visit the Tate now, and I'm going to drink from my flask. Would you care to join me?" Baptiste pauses for a moment. He raises his eyebrows, prodding for an answer.

"Another time."

My uncle, Willis, meets me at the Tube station. I am in Enfield, North London. Uncle Willis takes me on a scenic tour: John Keats studied at Clarke's Academy; the Enfield market, which dates back to the fourteenth century; and the famous gold post office.

My Uncle Willis works in the military, and it's top secret. And top secret is not sexy. My niece and nephew, Elaine and Casper, mope around the house and scream, "Dad's job is top secret!" I am neither curious nor inclined to entertain what "top secret" means. But *my* lack of interest piques *his* interest. He turns, unpretentious, and casually lights a cigarette in the kitchen, meaning to say ... anyone can find out, so why bother ask?

I tell Casper and Elaine I am a writer. Casper begins to laugh uncontrollably. Despite only being six years old, I feel a little perturbed by his rebuff. I look at my aunt and uncle for some support, and my Aunt Alice is too busy practicing the dice-cut for her cookbook video. My Uncle Willis is taking the cookbook far too seriously; he might sell his videographer skills later.

I roll up my sleeves as I begin to speak.

"I'm writing about a young man who once lived in London. And decides to end his life."

"God was supposed to help him with those thoughts!" said Casper.

"That's right, lad."

"What were his reasons to upset God?" asked Elaine.

Suddenly, I was in the grip of an existential crisis. The "does God exist?" question arises in the conversation. Strangely, my memory of Angel suddenly disappears. I am fighting cascading winds, and now I feel a little awkward in front of my family, for they have answered the question that Angel has avoided to ask. Why did he take his own life? Why did he choose to die when it was a choice for God to answer. I feel no compunction to defend Angel. I renege on my convictions, and feel more than ever a need to defend his choices, but I do not know enough about him to say why at this point. That uncertainty is rather refreshing and certainly sufficient enough to provide my family a promising answer.

"Oh well, he was probably tired of God not showing him enough guidance. He acted on his own."

"I think he should have finished university before he decided to be a schoolmaster."

"Yeah, maybe that's right."

They never admitted the reason for the sudden change in attitude. But I certainly did not want to risk looking like Cousin Eddie from *National Lampoon's Vacation*. I choose to leave.

I book a room at the Holiday Inn in Central London. The room is considerably smaller than the one in Winnipeg or else my B&B in New York. The furniture emits impermanence. It lacks the sense of vacation how we do it in the good ol' USA. You feel like you're staying in a cramped elevator. Any sense of freedom becomes the urgency to dress and go somewhere else. A jog; now hustle down for breakfast; check some emails; you're already late, and the concierge is wondering why you haven't asked for a taxi by now.

The Full Moon, an English pub, is famous for surviving the Great London Fire. It is a battle for the barman each night, for the waiters and waitresses, for the undecided crowd. A choice place for fine dining or to maximize joy with copious amount of drinking. It is a place to improvise, to live life rapturously and joyfully.

Angel looks glumly towards the street. A couple stops and examines the menu board in the window. Another couple—in matching leather jackets (tacky)—stops. Very few of the peripatetic players outside come inside, but there is some serious talk going on, bigger than the action happening inside the kitchen.

He orders coconut and red-lentil dahl. Baptiste sits at the bar and acts rather sullen, leaning his elbows on the dark brown bar and smiling mischievously.

"There is always something to do," said Baptiste.

"That's right. And not enough time to study."

Angel reaches to shake Baptiste's hand. The two men easily discard any normal London protectionist attitudes quickly.

Angel could feel the weight on his shoulders. Things were coming too easy for Baptiste. He has a light air about him. A gentle smile and shimmering eyes. And quite adept at starting a conversation in any context and looking adorably confident. These are all things Angel is lacking. Instead, Angel is forcing a smile or doubting his words. A lack of etiquette stands out. Angel scratches the ground with the sole of his shoe. He assumes he will find his place eventually. He squares up to Baptiste and begins to speak. He coughs a little to clear his throat.

"You accompanied someone?" asked Angel.

"Inès." Baptiste tilted his head as he spoke.

Baptiste is more than willing to obliterate any proper introductions by mentioning Inès's name. Moreover, Baptiste adds a cheeky smile to indicate his close relationship with Inès. The irregular facial expression is lost on Angel, who continues to find his feet. And now that they've broken the ice, Angel is ready to advance through the coarse exchange because, as is quite obvious to anyone, any type of exchange with Baptiste is rather torturous and dramatic.

"I'm from Canada," said Angel.

"It's only London. As a Frenchman, the beauty fades very quickly on me. Sometimes I think I would have made a better murderer here than a student."

"Yeah."

"That was a joke." Baptiste lights a cigarette.

He gets a Canadian flag tattoo on his chest, but with the twist of a golden twine. They go to a pub and decide to go out dancing. They are all on the dance floor: bumping, bodies, shrieks and hollers, and countless cycles back to the bar. At one point, each one has a bronzed London flame, in a pink-spaghetti strap dress, on his arm. They offer funny apologies and a final dart to one last bar.

Klein decides to break from the group; his expression switches from sad to happy.

Klein's mother, Carmen, attends our meeting at the Holiday Inn, and she stammers and twitches at Klein's sudden stroke of passion.

"It hasn't stopped," said Klein.

"What?" I replied.

"... we killed it that night."

London is a stark contrast from Angel's time in New York. He recalls the overpowering stench of the New York subway stations—or a homeless man marching down Broadway, pulling a cart, and one up front, with plastic bottles overflowing at each pothole. A cacophony of horns, and screams in various dialects: "Get outta the way!"

But inside the confines of the College London campus, there is a sense of conviviality to learning that exceeds anything he has seen before.

The auditorium holds one hundred students comfortably. The room has a gentle downward slope leading to a large overhead. A huge floor-to-ceiling thick window fills one side of the auditorium, with a multi-changing courtyard and an impressive English garden and fountain stand in the middle. A sense of invincible swoons the class.

Angel loosens his wry smile and admits this is home. He tightens the strap on his knapsack and finds a seat in the middle. A group of hip Arab men in aqua and beige head dress sit off to the side. Everyone nods a polite hello.

Angel flips through pictures on his mobile phone. Mostly of Leah in various states of intoxication. He deletes at least forty of these. Pictures of joints in various shapes. His dad in a Black face; Cameron in drag. His father, again in drag. A sense of shame. Not anger, but just witness to the classic white privilege; moronic humor. You know, those on the brink of either madness or fantasies of a murder/suicide. If it were not for immigrants entering Canada, to effectively elbow the inbred whites out, the government would still be doling our parcels of land.

Professor Matias Luiz is at times disarming and generous. At other times, he appears highbrow and invincible. He stands proudly behind the College London brand. In such a state, he becomes invincible for any complex ideas and bookish concepts. He sinks his mind around a great many things, in this state, and soon appears as the reason winner.

His first and only marriage is rather unorthodox. He purchases an apartment and soon discovers that, each night, it is overrun with prostitutes. He is in the habit of sweeping up needles each morning. But his curiosity gets the best of him. After a late show (*The Life of Pi*) he meets Nora in the "land of milk and honey" (according to his debonair real-estate agent). Soon he is holding the lid of a Rubbermaid garbage can and acting like a Roman warrior, engaging in all sorts of sordid affairs.

Nora stops working the courtyard, but cuddling and watching movies upstairs becomes intolerable (the memories are too overpowering). He wants to sell the apartment and start over. But nothing can fix their relationship. Nora likes her independence. Professor Luiz has been a little jittery since, thinking he resembles a character from a Lars von Tier movie.

Professor Luiz wears a reddish shirt and a green tie; an impressive light brown suit (sheen, wide lapel). His shirt focusses the class—as much as his erudite style and exquisite use of English. His face is smooth; small black moustache; black hair on the sides; a round and polite bald head.

"We've got a lot of territory to cover. Tell me the difference between economics and macroeconomics? Right, the former: customer behavior, the firm, markets, demand and supply. The latter, everything else: banking, business cycles, trade, the Philips curve, lots more."

Instinctively, Angel turns in his seat and smiles at Baptiste and Inès, who sit behind him.

"This guy is supposed to be a real genius," said Baptiste.

"Yeah, I hope it doesn't get in the way."

"What else?" asked Professor Luiz.

"Sir?" said Angel.

Angel looks around to see if the professor is looking at

anyone else.

"In macroeconomics?"

All eyes are on Angel.

"Aggregation, economic growth, general equilibrium."

"You've read the syllabus, I can see."

There are few instances of having nothing to say, or knowing how to behave. Ultimately, a good book, movie, or recipe for a drink, is a precursor for their engagements. And conflict turns into animated discussion about the said conditions of their meetings anyway: the importance of Marcel Proust; whether Dennis Hopper is a better director or actor; the painstaking process of how to make spring rolls; and, of course, how to mix a martini.

Inès comes from Nice, the South of France. She is very quiet and intellectual. Baptiste is from Rouen, is exuberant and obsessed with British culture. Angel fills out the third leg of the triumvirate. He holds a sports injury that otherwise could have led to a golf date with Roethlisberger. Winnipeg has the cultural weight of a piece of coal, save for Winnie the Pooh or Margaret Lawrence, or the famous Hitchcock reference in *The 39 Steps*.

They are both married, whereas Baptiste—obstinate to the core with his wife, Viola—has not found the time to engage a lawyer to finalize the divorce. Each one is physically fit and spends an inordinate amount of time drooling over fashion trends.

I rent a conference room at College London. I wear my Florida Gators jumper. Inès plays with her white gold bracelet, while Baptiste speaks on his gold-encased mobile phone and negotiates where to meet for drinks with friends. Angel remains fresh on their minds, however—not so much as a friend who dies tragically, but as a pillar of their comedy routine and an integral part of their daily life. Not to mention that he was the cause for Inès and Baptiste's eventual breakup, although Baptiste denies anything happened. Inès asks if I am enjoying my time in London. I reply: "I'm rather confused by Angel's willingness to drop out of college, unless the Professor and Angel had something going on?"

Her face transforms into anger, annoyance, and she feels nauseous. The room turns quiet; everyone now believes I am lame in bed.

Baptiste and Inès rent a flat on Orchard in central London. A brick-front, three-storey gem, with a tiny courtyard and iron fence. By all accounts they are living a life of privilege. The top-end postcode is replete with newly renovated structures, with a non-stop exchange of European luxury cars that line the traditional street. It is the floral deliveries, a flat screen in bubble wrap in the hallway, or else, one room cordoned off as a "project room." A stack of paintings or works by College London students that trigger random thoughts about the importance of markets and politics.

Inès and Baptiste finish talking with Professor Luiz. Angel reviews some class notes. As the two are about to leave, Baptiste stops and slams a postcard of a giant olive fizzing over the side of a champagne flute in front of Angel. The flip side shows their home address. Inès looks over Baptiste's shoulder and shouts:

"Big party, Angel!"

It was a delicious mixture of naïve sensibilities and

good music. Inès and Baptiste hire a set of twin female DJs. The turntables are set up in the middle of the room.

Professor Luiz wears a poor-fitting blue suit. His white dress shirt has circles of perspiration. He stuffs a brown tie into his chest pocket and bites his lip as he makes introductions.

Inès goes into the middle of the dance floor, raises her arms and starts to dance. The young professor unwittingly makes a move on an impressionable first year student. Or just being here, the very handsome invitation. And Baptiste (so easily outmanoeuvred) and the countless gentlemen like Angel (the lumps), who hold a weighty crush on the hostess. The flippant Professor Luiz looks towards Angel: "Don't mention this to anyone!"

They decide to slip away for a drink. The professor makes a silly comment and a funny face. Inès tracks her hand into the side of Baptiste's retro Guess jeans. They speak tenderly, loudly once more, as the party roars.

"Professor Luiz?" said Angel.

"Yes?"

"I didn't expect to see you here." Angel places his beer down on the hallway table.

"I'm always prowling the streets for Brexiteers and off-campus parties: cream of the crop."

Professor Luiz goes over to the window and lights a cigarette. Angel follows close behind.

"I quite enjoyed your discussion." Angel takes a quick swig of his beer.

"Aggregation."

"Yes, that was me."

Suddenly, Professor Luiz looks at the crowd on the dance floor, with no flair to leave this place.

Angel is a little glossy-eyed at being at the same party

with an author from St. Martin's Press. He rubs his eyes as he takes a drag off his cigarette. He holds his beer in an awkward sort of way.

The two men look each other over. Angel recalls his first meeting with Baptiste, and how awkward that moment felt, and he refuses to let it happen again. To be fair, Professor Luiz is a veteran in human psychology anyway. He is an old hat at reading people. A story like *Oleanna* is blue cheese on a Ritz cracker for this guy. Indeed, Angel takes a stab to make a first good impression, anything to prevent the professor from having any after thoughts about Angel's nature.

"I cannot quite get over what the little terror, Germany, did last century," said Professor Luiz.

"That makes a lot of sense." Angel nods in agreement.

"I don't want any part of Europe where Germany gets a piece of the pie. I'd like to see Britain leave the EU." Professor Luiz pours himself a shot of tequila.

"Oh, yes."

"In any case lad, food for thought." Professor Luiz takes a shot of tequila.

Angel walks through the dance floor and finds the bar.

"I'm sorry. Je suis désolé."

"Tu parles français. C'est bon, Angel." Inès removes a thread from the front of Angel's shirt.

"Un petit peu."

"I'm sorry. I left my coat in here and I'm about to leave."

He finds Alpha Books on Portsmouth Street. The corner entrance has two portable shelf units on rollers, full of modernist and avant-garde titles. Inside, the walls are plastered with mini posters of Edith Warton, James

Baldwin, Proust, Shakespeare, and Salmon Rushdie.

He tugs at the bottom of his denim shirt. He admires his grey suede boots. He gently tucks his hands into the rough beige canvas Carharrt vest.

"Funny finding you here," said Angel.

"I love walking through the bookstore. Even the children's section." Inès smiles and slowly walks away.

She wears a loose-fitting red top and baggy pants, and a thick leather belt. An expensive and hard-to-find pair of Nike Air Force Ones. She pinches the bottom corner of her glasses and gently lowers her head towards Angel's feet.

"Comfort food."

Angel uses his hands to mimic that he is eating something.

"Ç'est comme la nourriture du comfort."

Their eyes meet, and neither one has enough clout to make the first move. Instinctively, they feel the excitement of the other and are fully entitled to the other's faults at sharing too much. Their sole obsession is to please each other physically. Angel is resigned at making mistakes, but he insists on being one with Inès.

Suddenly Inès dislikes the boy crush, the infatuation, or even the weird gawk from a courtly stranger on a sidewalk in London. But the butterflies ... the butterflies are gnawing at her insides.

"Tu recruit for the movement."

"Yes, and..."

"Ça m'énerve. C'est toujours quelque chose avec son Brexit. Ça m'énerve."

Inès lights a cigarette and slams the lighter down on the counter.

They each admire the surroundings.

"Would you like to go to a café?" asked Angel.

I sit inside the lobby of the Resort Inn. Off to the side is a waiting area, with two oversized faux leather grey couches and a large glass table, with a yellow flower arrangement.

Baptiste wears sporty/casual, PSG nylon jacket, and ripped jeans. He pulls at the cords of his jacket like he is in an exercise video. Inès jacks the corner of her mouth back, and crosses her legs, her gold heels and buckle, and Chanel chain purse glitter.

Baptiste's demeanor has not changed since his time with Inès. Today's meeting is no different. Inès dislikes Baptiste's anecdotes, and Baptiste favors the view that Inès's recollection is naïve and falsely reports what was really going on in their lives. In other words, Inès could not possibly have fallen for Angel.

I recall meeting Baptiste outside of College London. We are meeting to discuss a few items, and a young woman walks past in an Arsenal jersey.

"It is a bad omen to let a beautiful woman pass by and not try and improve your life exponentially."

I am saying to speak up! Baptiste's feelings don't count for a hill of beans, given that, well, she has feelings for Angel.

She possesses the detachment for Angel that Leah has, who sometimes appears confused by my questions. Her eyes are shaky, her smile authentic, and the discourse about her past is always churning in her mind. She puts her hand in her hair, sculpts the back of her satiny bob, mostly warning me about Baptiste's state of mind. Despite a successful and growing family (an overpowering part of her life) she continues to think of Angel; her memory for Angel grows. Her legal battles with Fanny have enhanced Angel's memory evermore.

Angel and Inès walk leisurely down Portugal Street; eventually they arrive at a busy four-lane intersection, the 4200. The come upon Pret a Manger. From the outside it looks like a McDonald's or a Burger King. Inès bends down and rolls up her ripped jeans. Angel removes his red Yankees tuque, and softly taps Inès on her lower back. They venture inside.
"You have almond-shaped eyes."

Angel holds Inès in his arms, and she falls backward into the open fridge. They laugh as they embrace on the hard floor. They reach the bedroom, and have a humorous shouting match as to whether to pull the curtains closed.
"I'm not competing for you." Angel walks away and decides to sit down on a chair beside the window.
"No."
Inès walks over to Angel and sits on his lap.
"I'm tired, just from being so far from home," shrugs Angel, peering at a taxi on the street below.
"Baptiste is nothing to me," said Inès.
"I have a paper due Monday."
Angel gets up and starts to organize his desk where he will spend the night reading and writing.
"Yes, it will all flutter away eventually, like the leaves. Look at the European leaves from your silly Canadian eyes."
Inès finds her purse and gets ready to leave.

Professor Luiz comes up the street and admires the scattering leaves.

"Oh no. Him," said Inès.

Angel abandons Inès, and focusses on Professor Luiz. Inès is not impressed.

"Professor Luiz. Hello, sir."

"Perhaps some lunch tomorrow? If you can make it. I need to discuss some urgent matters with you."

Porfessor Luiz continues to walk down the street.

Inès reaches over and takes Angel's arm, but Angel clings to Professor Luiz's words so closely that he hardly notices her presence.

"What does *he* want?" Inès grabs Angel's arm.

"He wants me to help him with his political goals."

Inès can tell that Angel is obsessed with the prospect of an important friendship. Inès stops Angel in the middle of their walk.

"Kiss me."

Angel gently holds Inès in his arms, and he appears clingier than anyone she has ever kissed. She keeps pace to be the same.

"It was a lovely kiss. Much better than Baptiste. Hold my hand." Inès holds Angel's arm, searching for his hand.

There's something endearing about him: a mix of humor and touch of Somerset Maugham. Yes, a youngish man who sits, slumped over, and seems as dispossessed and disenchanted as anyone. And, dare I say, how many of us really care about a first-year university student anyway? But Professor Luiz takes an interest in all his students, and his positive connections makes all of us feel a little guilty.

Professor Luiz recalls their first meeting. He schools Angel on some of the realities of Brexit, including the UK assuming a rather vulnerable military position.

Professor Luiz remains loyal to Madilyn and Cameron. In other words, Professor Luiz sees Angel as the great hope, a steadfast partner, to take their working relationship to new and exciting career ends.

Angel meets Professor Luiz at the faculty cafeteria. The waitress is heavyset, with thick ankles, and wears a red dress. Her face is plump with deep-set green eyes, and dark hair with a cowlick. She is accessorized in kiosk earrings, and a street-vendor leather bracelet.

An old colleague once blocks the presiding PM because "rules will be rules." The waitress is obstinate. She gulps some air and grips her heavy sides. Meanwhile, Angel surveys the cafeteria: hundreds of light pine chairs, maybe a few thousand square feet, white tables. They find a table overlooking the busy street below. The waitress recommends the *plat du jour*.

Unlike Socrates, who denies his accusers, Professor Luiz comes clean about stretching an olive branch to Angel, but admits it is more like an olive farm, with handlers on the side to wipe his ass. It is a chance of a lifetime, and only a fool would pass it over.

"You can leave now."

"I don't get it."

"Vis-à-vis our little talk. There's a lot more to say about Brexit than what we discussed."

Professor Luiz starts to roll up the sleeves of his shirt.

"I woke up in cold sweats. The separation from the EU has nothing to do with Germany! It's about fairness and equality. And establishing a strong British trade agreement. Just a proportional, or equal, deal."

"Okay."

"If we can find weaknesses to stay in the EU, then

sovereignty becomes an attractive concept. But that's not what I believe."

"I get it, sir."

"Just get away from the idea that this is something to do with pride, or ethnicity, or history."

As he smacks the edge of the table, a very calming trust envelops the two men. It is a beat of approval to continue their friendship.

"But you made me say the last thing I wanted to say."

"I made no such suggestion."

"You did, lad. The EU is an economic prison. That's the final word."

Angel pushes his side plate away, with the untouched pickle.

"Order a beer, lad. I say all of this because I am going to make a very strategic move shortly, with respect to my career."

The two men are becoming fast friends. It is the last thing Angel would ever have expected. The professor takes an interest in Angel for the simple reason that Angel can carry on a conversation. Angel asks some tough questions about Brexit. Professor Luiz is used to quick answers on the subject matter. Or else long-winded diatribes from precocious students who write with the singular aim of obtaining an A. Angel huffs and puffs, running in all directions, or counterattacks, or else tries to disprove anything that the professor says. Strangely, like great foes in a sports arena, the professor finds his opponent useful for his own goals. He breaks for the end zone with the aim that Angel ... cannot do anything else but follow.

"I'm thinking about stepping down from teaching and work full-time on Brexit, and I want you to be my wingman. You'll be in charge of speech writing."

Some feather-filled couch cushions are overturned. The Monet and Van Gogh reproductions have been removed from the wall, leaving a rather nasty tan line. Lamps are scattered every which way. Lots of stacks of books. And umbrellas. He's hosting a successful garage sale. But he is anxious. Any comfort and serenity are gone.

Angel is undecided whether to take an interest in any of the professor's possessions or treat them as garage-sale items. The professor is leaving his former life and setting sail on a new voyage. But the professor also displays his doubts about his decision. His belongings assume a safe place. Each pile acts like a buoy in treacherous waters, where someday the books will once again glean on a bookshelf. The professor will be seated at his desk, hulking over complex questions on political science, and no doubt wrestling with a passage from John Stuart Mill, who, in the professor's mind, makes much more sense than anything Angel could ever say.

"The world is turning fast. Look around: boxes full of books—we're going to change the face of democracy."

"I brought a copy of a cheque so you can make direct deposits."

Professor Luiz holds his glasses on his forehead as he comes around the table.

"He shoots, he scores?!"

"I noticed you had posted everyone's marks but mine?" asked Angel.

"I thought we were a team?"

"What?" Angel scratches his chin.

"I'll pay you enough to live, and travel costs. In return

you're going to write speeches for some of the UK's most interesting politicians."

"I read in a book that wages have not increased significantly."

"The EU has put the people in the poorhouse. There's no chance of wages ever increasing. Not under the current deal."

Angel goes over to the window and looks at the students walking around the campus. He turns around and raises his eyebrows, waiting for what comes next.

"The EU creates an atmosphere of instability, which presents the impossibility of wages to increase."

No one obsesses about the coursework, just how their mark appears on their transcript. Angel is no different. Professor Luiz is familiar with the one-on-one battles, and he tends to succeed at making sure his students reach their goals. But this is different, Angel will assume an irregular offer.

Baptiste is quite sure it was an old film noir (*Double Indemnity*) that they watched. But Inès is positive it was *Blade Runner 2049*. How could you make such a blatant oversight?

The sign outside the Peacock Theatre says *Blade Runner 2049*. The—mostly university—crowd enters and takes their seat.

Baptiste styles a trench coat with a white pocket on the back, open shirt and dark dress pant. Inès turns to Baptiste. She wears her hair up, tights, with a loose-fitting white blouse and oversized cardigan. Angel sits in the back corner of the spacious movie theatre. He wears denim, and motorcycle boots.

Angel considers going over and sitting with his friends. But he decides to remain in his seat. Baptiste and Inès, given their sophistication anyway, are romantic enough to forgive him. After all, Baptiste is still content at being close to his girl.

Friends do remind you of, and tell you, how nice you look—or conversely when you deserve a compliment. He looks at the nape of their neck, at their discreet, cinematic poses, the sounds of their clothing, at Baptiste's colossal moves at grabbing Inès's attention.

Baptiste disappears. Angel throws down his popcorn. He grips the dark blue velvet and makes his way towards Inès.

"Baptiste will be back soon."

"I want to see you?" Angel gently touches the back of Inès shoulder.

"Oh, Angel" Inès reaches for Angel's hand. She finds his hand and makes a firm grip.

"Give me your number?"

Inès fumbles with her mobile phone. She opens her notebook.

"I intend to make my mark here, with anyone who will join me."

"Go, Angel. On se parlera bientôt. Vite. Baptiste arrive. À bientôt." Inès reaches over and kisses Angel on the cheek

Inès is an independent woman. And politics justify most of her choices. Her relationship with Baptiste is enigmatic and complex. She manages their relationship on the weight of its complex structure. Yet, whenever she meets Angel, or Baptiste disappears for any length of time, she recognizes her need to change.

Inès stands in the middle of the narrow street and

hollers Angel's name. He offers her an orange scone and tea. She remains tickled at hollering someone's name at the top of her lungs.

She makes no sign of anything sexual. But she turns and their eyes match, their unexpecting lips touch. Somehow, they each acknowledge this feels right. All their doubts are erased as the kissing moves easily to what comes next.

*

Several weeks pass, and Angel is invited over to Inès and Baptiste's apartment. Next, Inès takes everyone to the community garden, where they have coffee. The tension builds when Inès places a flower on Angel's leg. Baptiste snidely exclaims they should build a green house. The situation deflates, given Baptiste's recent forte into home renovation.

Baptiste wears an old pair of overalls and muscle shirt and walks around with his arms raised (outfitting the apartment with pit-hair, and carpentry chic). Inès moans: tu es macho, et surtout sexy, oui, je t'aime.

There is some unintelligible bickering. And longish stares at each other. Baptiste goes from room to room searching for nothing in particular while tidying. It feels awkward, clinical.

Angel looks out the window and sees his empty Styrofoam cup in the community garden. An elderly man in a checkered jacket, picks up the cup, and turns and stares tempestuously at Angel.

They express displeasure after Angel speaks. They create a hostile environment for someone who is not French. But Baptiste senses his tendency to act jealous and vindictive. He finds her eyes, his evil and safe place, and buries any guilt or responsibility, and insists he is not part of anyone's games.

Angel springs up and glosses over the backsplash and beats his chest at Baptiste's workmanship. They dance a folk turn or two of mad joy, until Inès enters the kitchen with sharpened teeth.

"I like Professor Luiz."

"So, he can exploit you. He merely likes the company of young boys."

"Or maybe he is telling the truth?" Angel puts his arm over Inès shoulder.

"But what happens after the referendum?"

"What do you mean?"

"You'll be out of a job?"

Baptiste gets up and leaves the room allowing the two to speak once more in more authentic tones and inflections. A sense of deception enters their friendship, and an uncertain future holds steady.

I come upon Angel's apartment. I buzz the landlord.

Mr. Houghes is a small man who wears a long woollen harlequin jacket with missing buttons. He has one arm. His face is friendly, with a large bulbous nose, and aqua, soft lubricant eyes. He is bald and has a little tail which is tied with a dirty elastic. He hints that I should give him some pocket money, but I don't. We enter into polite conversation about Angel.

After Angel dies, Dougald McClock, a conservative MP from Harrow East, eager to promote his political reputation at inane times, writes a reflective piece for *The Guardian* on Brexit, and mentions Angel. In a nutshell, he memorializes Angel as an inadvertent soldier for the cause but is a victim of wild sex orgies on the campaign trail. It includes a picture of himself and Fanny and Angel at a pub. It looks and smells salacious.

I exclaim he is barking up the wrong tree. They are more interested in pulling the UK out of Europe.

"Oh, good!"

Mr. Houghes is overcome with exhaustion. He motions that I go up to the top floor alone. I peek over the staircase and hear some Caribbean accents, possibly Jamaican.

"He was a delight and carried my groceries. He even gave me his number for any chores we might have for him. Just think, all you remember is that he was a touch odd."

"That's right—pure love, that boy, and who knows what we're stuck with next."

"If you don't get the door, it might be me."

Angel is so high up in the sky that lugging *The New York Times International Edition, The Times,* home each day is burdensome. The view from the top-floor window is obstructed by the overhang from the window below. The view stretches into the far distance on either side. A suicide note appears safe from this vantage point.

The sloping ceiling is perfectly angled for a desk and small bookcase. It remains studious enough for anyone to pursue their academic goals.

Professor Luiz knocks at the door.

"Angel?"

Angel opens the door. Professor Luiz holds a mischievous stare.

"Sir?"

"Yes, Angel, let me in."

Angel looks around his apartment and realizes this is no place to host a guest.

"Have you had any breakfast, sir?"

They sit in a little café at the corner of the street. It has a black and white marble tiled floor. The marble tables feel cold, except when the food arrives. Professor Luiz warns him their relationship would be unorthodox at the best of times. We should learn to depend on each other when we least expect it.

A young man enters the café and approaches the counter. He slams down his croissant and complains about the quality.

"It tastes off."

It is commonplace to see complaints at the restaurant. Complaints about the food never seems to reflect poorly on the restaurant, as though it is immune to any criticism. However, it might also be that it has become so arrogant about its service that an occasional poor dish or bad pastry gets served inadvertently to customers. But there are no checks and balances to help the customer per se. The typical response is just a rolling of the eyes and a quick exchange at whatever the customer wants. Today is no different. Professor Luiz is unimpressed about the complaint—taking the side of the restaurant—which shows a cold side of his personality. Angel does not understand why the customer appears so angry over such a frivolity.

"Just replace it."

Angel is unable to defend the young man. It works to set the tone.

A rather cunning young professor on the prowl. He studies philosophy at Columbia; his father works as an executive at the UN. His first couple of weeks in Manhattan are a complete write-off. His father remains adamant, however: you are among the tribe that made all the Vietnam movies you love so much. Later, he returns to London, lives with his mother, and resumes his studies at Oxford, where he graduates with a PhD in economics.

"I've quit the Academy." Professor Luiz removes a flask and takes a quick nip of scotch.

"I've still got two more exams."

"Do you not feel the energy?" Professor Luiz offers Angel the flask, but Angel politely declines.

"No. I feel..."

"The British wave?"

"Sir, I want a French girlfriend, and a degree from a good English university. I have no weight with the British people."

Professor Luiz ignores Angel's comments. It is a slip of the tongue, or an idealist with too much slack. Yet Professor Luiz is motivated to continue. There's a maniacal aspect about their plan, and here Angel is simply mouthing off some pent-up anxiety. However, Professor Luiz sees the process churning in Angel's eyes and, despite not hearing what he wants to hear,

Professor Luiz feels more motivated than ever.

"You've been thinking about it, lad?"

"Maybe." Angel nods his head, saying he is all-in.

"We're going to start at one end of the country and go to the other. We've got government support. Stay at the finest hotels and eat the finest food."

"I guess so." Angel begins to crack a smile.

"Go out and buy a suit."

"I told my dad today about our plan, and he hung up."

Ariana speaks with a Greek accent. She wears wide navy-blue pants and a yellow and gold blouse. She has very long wrists and lovely pinkish fingernails. She wears a gold chain.

She likes Angel and acts overly suggestive: pubs, little walks—but Angel stands his ground. He heckles with funny looks and bursts of laughter.

"You got four A's and one B+."

"What did I get a B+ in?"

"Professor Luiz, who is no longer with us. He's been replaced by Schwartz, who is from Edinburgh."

"I'm not coming back in January."

Ariana is not meddling, but she obliges—given, well, the importance of College London. She reaches her arms across the wicket and holds Angel's palm between her thumb and slender, lenticular index finger.

Angel sees the touch as something more authentic than anything he has ever experienced before. The decision to drop out of university has no weight; his family is absent from his mind, for he looks deep into the eyes of some stranger and has no compulsion to let go. But the queue of students calls, or the other clerks stare at Angel to see what he wants. Angel acts protectively towards Ariana, veering on consoling her more than his predicament demands.

"May I ask why?" Ariana awaits an answer, even though her question was unnecessary.

Angel puts his papers inside his knapsack but shows no signs of leaving.

"I had a windfall of an opportunity."

"Professor Luiz has taken you under his wing. Am I right?" Ariana stamps some documents, and then flips the stamp on the counter.

"Perhaps something like that."

"Don't you think you're going to drag the UK into some unknown abyss? And act so indifferent, like it's some rail-pass-through-Europe experience?"

"Right. For now, that's exactly how I feel."

"Just watch it. But Luiz is a rare one; he'll do you right." Ariana smiles; she resumes stamping the documents.

"College London will always be here."

Angel looks at Ariana and he clings to the hope she is wrong. But deep down he senses she might be right.

Angel stops in front of a large storefront window and admires the latest fashions. He feels uplifted by his choices, for his new career offers opportunities, for a new life. He stops and listens to a modish busker who plays guitar, mostly from The Who's repertoire: a loud drumbeat and inordinate focus on guitar riffs. It occurs to him that he is well adapted to his new home.

Sitting in his apartment a daily routine emerges: a review of *The Times, Daily Mail, Daily Telegraph* and, occasionally, *The Sun*; download articles from the internet; the memorization of British factoids; and a constant review the PM's stand on issues, and always finding a pro-Brexit response.

Angel cracks a circumspect window for a little fresh air, when he sees Professor Luiz walking up the chummy street.

He offers the professor a cup of coffee, with two sugar cubes on the side. Collapsed in a beanbag chair, he holds the cup like he is posted up low on an NBA court. Angel sits on a folded metal chair opposite Professor Luiz, with the front window to his right. Professor Luiz can look at either Angel or the well-mannered Indian family in the apartment across the street.

Professor Luiz assumes the shadowy father-figure.

"You're not writing a speech! You're forcing me to be an editor!" stormed Professor Luiz.

"Okay."

"Time is of the essence. All right? Get it right, Angel."

"Yeah."

"Okay. None of this Irish border nonsense. Or sovereignty. Don't spark any discussions for the Irish and Scots to get hot. Or the Welsh. Or whatever comes up. Let the MPs worry about the minutiae."

Things start to get real when they meet MPs at Westminster. And later, in goofy restaurants close to Tube stations. Suddenly, the two are experts on Brexit. They charge a handsome fee.

The MPs open their wallets because they don't want to appear undecided or uninformed about the intricacies of Brexit.

Dougald McClock is a Conservative MP from Harrow East. He welcomes Professor Luiz and Angel to Queen Anne's Gate, a spacious second-floor apartment in St. James Park part of London. They sit on a hard leather couch, while Mr. McClock stands and munches on a toasted sardine and cucumber sandwich.

"Never mind polling or sending out email blasts—and don't even think of the Royal Mail service. Instead, do what Malcolm X did: stand on a soapbox outside any Tube station, and just talk until you start to make sense. People will eventually come and listen."

"Brilliant."

They rent a medium-size community club. It has a small stage at the front. The room is standing room only.

Mr. McClock inspects the posters that Angel ordered.

The EU threatens British sovereignty
The EU strangles the UK with regulations
The EU favors corporate interest
The euro is shite

Mr. McClock works the crowd. His interactions are real and vital, and the burden of preparation soon disappears. During the MP's interactions, he spots Angel and Professor Luiz and treats them like they are fellow members of government. Professor Luiz hands Angel a glass of wine to keep him standing.

"The difference between the weather and the current economic crisis is that the UK has a choice to improve its health. Why would someone choose to stay in a relationship where they are taxed disproportionately and not offered anything in return? Why should the UK dole out huge amounts to the EU when it cannot afford to spend on its own infrastructure? Why should the population's interest be tailored to improve Europe, when for centuries the UK proved it could succeed on its own? How does the EU foster a united UK—or a healthy UK, for that matter? Lower class and the middle class have not seen any wage increases in decades. When the UK *wasn't* part of the EU, they saw much better profits."

Professor Luiz and Angel are about to leave when a couple of anti-Brexiteers block them on the street.

"Who gives you the right to spread a bunch of lies to the working-class people?" asked the protestor.

"What lies?"

"How about the UK is better off outside the EU?"

Angel and Professor Luiz sense a great divide emerging. They remain stoic: a single force against the anti-Brexit campaign. Angel's first instinct is to stop the man from approaching. Angel raises his arms in a violent manner. Everyone is a little stunned by Angel's knee-jerk reaction. Professor Luiz points angrily at the man. Next, Professor Luiz raises his briefcase and acts like he is going to throw it to the ground.

"That's what I believe."

"He knows better *because* he's Canadian; an impartial opinion matters," said Professor Luiz.

"I don't give a toss what some thrasher from Canada thinks."

"Oh, so you're suddenly an authority on Brexit?" Angel raises his fists in defiance.

"No wonder we're going to hell—you're not even from the bloody UK."

"I'm making my way, like everyone!"

Angel and Professor Luiz nod at the common understanding they can build on the little bit of acrimony. Angel neither resists the low blow nor entertains its malicious nature.

Angel arrives late at Lambeth North Tube station. He stares at the red-tiled firehouse knock-off and could reminisce about Winnipeg: the Osborne Village Firehouse.

Journal entry:

My life derives from this place. My great-grandparents once called these streets home. But the routine of an apprenticeship clash with the dream of the Canadian prairie and convinces his brother to join him, you know, to live in mud huts, stuffed with hay, on a section of land, each taking one hundred and sixty acres, and hopefully see each other every couple of months. They assume the farm duties for the next forty years.

Angel recognizes a full day of campaigning has come to an end. It's more than sharing a distilled drink and reinforcing vigorous political ideas: it's placing a log in the fireplace to reinforce bigger options, strengthen society—and now any insecurities are only for those who have a slightly different political bend.

Barbara, a Labour MP from London, wears a little red jacket and black blouse. Her hair is coiffed, set high on her head. She resembles something from a seventeenth century portrait studio. They spend a few civil moments together, enhancing each other's character. Everyone holds a pint and raises their drink.

At the College London library, in the centre, an elevator fleets students to an impressive library. Baptiste wears a leather jacket, and now he's miffed at Inès, who changes so dramatically. Angel appears and smiles, and feels uplifted by his London friends.

"So, what happened between you and Inès?" Baptiste looks like he is about to snap.

"My God man, what gave you that idea?"

"She's screamed your name during sex."

"Take some confidence pills." Angel smiles mischievously, but not in a way to antagonize Baptiste.

"Oh yes, especially now that you're a streetwalker."

"Wrong expression. I'm campaigning for Brexit." Angel covers his mouth, to stop from laughing.

"Besides, we've already been working with lots of MPs."

"Too bourgeois for me. Little British people think they are fancy, and they want to leave Europe."

"There might be some of that," added Angel.

Baptiste inspects some of Angel's scholarly texts.

"Look I'm working on a speech about Article 50. However, I need to study more about the World Trade Organization."

"I cannot believe any of this." Baptiste tosses his pen on the desk.

"I'm as qualified as anyone. The EU has sapped all of these special, thinking intellectuals on these issues into the ground. So, we make it up as we go along."

"So typically British: have to be on the firing line on every subject matter."

Angel pauses before speaking.

"How is Inès?"

"Quite good."

"Quite curious why my name was mentioned."

"I'm hardly offended. Although, if you're hiding something from me, let me know."

"A little blunt, Baptiste."

"Article 50 is your slam dunk. If you can get the MPs to get on board with that shite, France and the rest of the EU will give you a triumphant send-off." Baptiste grabs his pen off the desk and searches for a loose leaf of paper.

Angel misses on the enormity of Brexit. He still feels like he is holding the huddle, and Professor Luiz is making touchdowns. But Brexit stretches much further than a flush football field. It's World War II for the Brits. As well as Brits trying like hell not to sound-off how they really feel. It's for economic reasons, racist reasons, and—ultimately—British reasons. The latter is where the country feels well enough to close the blinds each night.

Journal entry:

I feel the Brits have a right to choose whether they want to be a part of the EU or not. I get the worry about Nationalism. The perceptions. But it's not about Nationalism, save for those who are interested in this historical dialectical approach. The UK is seeking out a better deal, and nothing more.

Kate Winners (a Labour MP from London with a short-haired Audrey Hepburn look and a preference for bow ties) calls in need of a peppy speech for a group of blue-collar types the next day.

"We don't want to trigger any socialist emotions; we merely need them to vote yes on Brexit."

"Oh yes, we can do that."

The fish cannery is not far from Billingsgate Market, employs about one hundred, and focusses on salmon, sardines, and white fish, when the price is right. Most of the stock arrives each morning around 3 a.m.

The employees are mostly in their forties. They wear jeans and jumpers, with logos like Gucci or Oxford, or else waffle shirts. They adjust to the well-dressed politician.

"There are some people who will like to tell you that the cost of regulation is offset by the money that the EU brings in. Regulation alone: we're looking at about thirty-five billion pounds sterling per year. The EU economics tell us that that brings in about sixty billion in revenue.

But don't they realize that the small-business owner doesn't care! The EU is trying to tell you how to run your business! You would have thought going out fishing, and stocking suppliers like Harrods's and Selfridges, was noble work. The employees deserve some credit, but instead you end up paying the EU out of your profits.

The group of employees are unanimous in supporting Brexit.

"The EU says: you have to insulate your building, improve the refrigeration, and so on and so forth. To sell a fillet of salmon, or canned salmon, we need to use a label that says this product contains fish. Do you know what that kind of label does to a mom-and-pop shop? Yeah, it tears a strip out of their profit line and keeps them up at night, unsure how to pay their employees and less likely to be creative and explore other business ventures because they don't know when the EU is going to hit them for more regulations and, essentially, hold back wages on the good British people. Now, do you think our Brexit plan is going to penalize the small-business owner? Or do you think we intend to help small business, deregulate, and put our products into luxury shops all over Europe?"

The crowd begins to jostle, clap, whistle, cheer, and finally give a thunderous cry of support.

The retreat is organized by a group Conservative MPs, who refuse to give their names. Professor Luiz will present two full days on issues related to Brexit, issues that are easy to understand yet remain intellectually rigorous. The conference is held at Blenheim Palace in Woodstock, Oxfordshire. A stone palace, built on three hundred acres of parkland. It is famous for its impressive library, organ, and being the birthplace of Sir Winston Churchill. Professor Luiz creates a two-day event that will crush any course syllabus at College London.

Trouble arises when two Russian attendees ambush Professor Luiz during the Q&A. Even Angel is itching to answer some of their questions. The two meddlers are ill-prepared for what comes next. Professor Luiz decides to tuck the FSB in once and for all. The gashing is irreversible, and the older one, with a straggly beard and expensive suit, must reach over and put his arm around his mate to help manage his breathing. The room turns cold. Day two is spent on the grounds, playing croquet and Frisbee.

Professor Luiz suggests they go to Brussels and see if they can offer their services to the opposite team. Angel feels the assurances sound better and better. How revolutionary it feels to enter university, and next be charting a country's future.

Inside the Palace of Westminster concepts are tailored to perfection and translated into press releases for the public. Or instead crafted into erudite speeches to discuss further in parliament. It's the place where thinking and action intersect. Or, where the thinking and hopes and wishes of parliamentarians turn into language for the people.

Pete Peterson, a Conservative MP from London, meets Professor Luiz and Angel at the entrance of Portcullis House. The office's decor is drab: panel lights and oily green carpet, and Ikea-like furniture. But, the view of Westminster is lovely.

They sit in a cramped office. Angel must stand beside

a large desk and act like he is comfortable and ready to share complex ideas.

"We're sitting with the big boys now."

"I know you can throw a football; give it up, son."

"I just don't know if it's right and proper that I'm in the middle of all of this?"

"I deleted the copy you sent me. "

Mr. Peterson holds a speech that Angel has written.

Angel waves his arms in disbelief. "You helped him out with this?" Mr. Peterson turns towards Professor Luiz for an answer.

"None of it, sir."

Angel raises his eyes; it sounds too rehearsed for such a heavy compliment.

"Well, that is all right!"

Alas, it is the moment Angel had been waiting for: namely, to receive some recognition for holding his own in the relationship. Angel has no reason to hold a stare on the distinguished MP, or else provide a gushing response from a compliment. Instead, he looks at Professor Luiz, who, upon recognition of Angel's shy nature, searches for some proper response to ensure Angel successfully sublimates the compliment into productive energy.

"We've been getting a lot of attention on the campaign trail so far," said Professor Luiz.

"Yes, then. I'll read this today. Let's get some lunch. "

"That's right, sir." Professor Luiz gets up from his seat and acts like the meeting is over.

Mr. Peterson comes around from his desk and shakes hands with his two special guests.

"We'll get you that working visa you're looking for."

Professor Luiz saunters down the halls of Westminster, a concrete floor that has been scurried over for centuries.

Even the stone benches look untouched by Father Time.

"You've written one that puts us in the end zone," screamed Professor Luiz.

"What's this?" Angel waves his arms in disbelief.

"Look around—it makes no difference what they think. The people are going to vote this one in."

London King's Cross has a giant mushroom sprouting in the middle, which octopuses into a shimmering blue ceiling. The modernism is obvious: high-tech royal blue contrasts with old brick, highlighting an old-meets-new dialectic.

It's a mixture of locals and tourists, and the architecture makes everyone look important. You can be a banker from Lloyds, carry a duffle bag, or be going to the gym, but the atmosphere puts a spell on you. Gangs of teenagers from Eastern Europe laugh and insult everyone who walks past, and soon they are full of excitement at the sheer number of coppers. Everyone tends to behave themselves, if not a little resentful at its magnificence.

Professor Luiz wears a stiff trench. His arms have a white stain of salt water. Angel wears a blue trench with lots of pockets and a tidy belt that ties at the back. They reach the platform, and set about walking along the clean cement, thickly painted iron pillars, the rounded skylight. It all feels rather historical as they find the train car to enter.

"I forgot something," said Professor Luiz.

Professor turns and looks towards the entrance of the station.

"I forgot my laptop. I'll meet you at the hotel."

Angel looks at the ceiling in a state of disbelief.

"I can't go without you!"

The train platform widens; the energy of the motley

commuters arouses Angel's senses. Growing up in Winnipeg, racism is at the tip of everyone's tongue. The downtown corps is alive and well, with zombie-like creatures, sometimes walking in groups. You soon realize the issue of poverty and homelessness is not for lack of jobs. Poverty is a race issue. The depths of poverty to which these people will descend ... the "hell" found in the Bible tastes like lukewarm tea.

The Black porter takes his ticket. The porter speaks with a Haitian accent and, truthfully, he could be part of the Royal Family. And how different from the CN, or trips to the US, where so much history is gripped by the people who work the trains. The differences are subtle, and just enough to trigger the comparison that racism is alive and well in the heart of London.

Georgina Petit wears a yellow ensemble: an aqua blouse, shiny pleather skirt, and black fishnet stockings The porter pushes a little buggy full of drinks and snacks. Exemplary opportunity for the young Frenchwoman and Angel to fiddle with each other's eyes. How quickly they share desperate looks and rehearse good habits while ordering.

"Something, sir?"

"Just a ginger ale. Chips ... I mean crisps, if you have some?"

Just as the train accelerates, it slows down. Many of the regulars crumple the sides of *The Times* and curse under their breath. Georgina takes no notice of the outskirts of London; her eyes are lost on Angel's consternation.

Journal entry:

She looked like some plastic plant at the bottom of my

betta aquarium. I was a little bitter at Professor Luiz for standing me up. Of course, I had some baloney sandwiches and Johnnie Walker. No doubt checking out the side show from the train would have been alright, but I thought we were going to discuss Plato's Republic. He seems to disappear at such decisive moment in my life. He's holding me back. He sees the world a little more room temperature than the rest of us. "I've forgotten something, lad."

Her mom and dad believe in mermaids.

"There's been an accident on the train, oui, un accident," said Angel.

"Ce n'est pas possible?"

Angel acknowledges the news. He recoils at not acting right, meeting the right emotion with the facts.

"Un suicide. C'est pourquoi nous avons arrêté."

A conductor enters the train and asks that everyone exit the train and stand on the platform.

"Do you want to go for une cigarette?" asked Georgina.

"I think I'll wait here."

Georgina has seen depths about the suicide that Angel does not see, and now he feels more confused about the situation. Georgina's disappearance appears to burden Angel further, highlighting his inability to see the callous nature of the situation. Her choices felt right, at leaving this place, and finding some other connection (no matter a taxi, shuttle, or hitch a ride). He looks up and down the long, neat platform and nods in resignation. Now the image of someone on the tracks appears in his mind. The sense of sharing something with the dead. This feeble life, save for the convenience of an open track to take away their pain. It's like a time lapse, full of light blurs.

The familiar and strange. Even the conductor seems lost in the frenzy. The platform fills up again.

Moment's pass, when—finally—the conductor signals they are ready to leave.

"We're ready for you, sir," said the conductor.

Angel points at the stairwell, leading towards the exit.

"What in the hell do you intend to do for that bloody French woman?"

"Excuse me?" The porter tries to seek an explanation from Angel's rather pestering cry.

There is no way to make any sense out of the situation. The porter has no real obligation to settle things with Angel. Angel had no reason to expect any resolution. Angel is a bystander, like everyone else. What business does Angel have to try and intervene in the first place? The porter has seen such attempts before, and immediately Angel is construed as nosy. The Good Samaritan law is provided the best answer the porter can muster.

"There is some French woman wandering about, not close to catching this train." Angel tugs at the lapels of his trench jacket.

"There are lots of shops down below; she's probably made other arrangements."

The two men assume their roles in quick manner.

"And smoking is not permitted," quavered the taxi driver.

"Right."

The taxi driver looks in the rear-view mirror, and Angel tries to hide from sight.

"I expect you're with the conference?"

"I am."

"I've travelled outside the UK. I had no troubles. I just prefer we keep it our own. I'm not saying we should stop people from coming—but let us make the decision, and not Brussels."

The taxi driver stops and stares at the front entrance long enough for Angel to see that they've arrived at their destination.

"It's only a job for me. What do I owe you?" Angel puts out some bills from his wallet.

"Fare's on me. Thank you, son." The driver stares at the front entrance as though he's arrived at his own personal destination, taking Angel's place.

"A free fare is a free fare. Let's hope we have better luck at meeting people."

Baptiste and I drink copious amounts of wine. At least three bottles, followed by a few beers. Jack Daniel's, I keep repeating, "My country, my country!" as we carouse down the narrow, historical streets.

He never appears drunk. He runs through traffic. His appetite for women is never-ending. My sincere approaches are boring and unjustified. We go to a *boîte noire* and now he makes out with an acquaintance, who becomes the centre of attention for the rest of the men at the bar. There is a deep sense of jealousy, watching him perform. Much of the frenzy tends to be about exploiting the ignoble and to find joy in the crevices of your entourage's fears.

Angel arrives at Baptiste and Inès's apartment with a bottle of wine. Baptiste has thrown out his Ikea desk. The "learning studio" is replete with Japanese carpets.

The night begins with a bottle of Bordeaux rosé in the

community garden. Later, a Greek restaurant. Salsa on the terrace. Then back to the apartment, smoke a joint, and listen to Marvin Gaye.

They act friendly *and* taciturn, for they are the last to complain of a possible friendship. They each recognize the limits of their personality and the difficulty of meeting people in London. So, Angel focusses on Baptiste's handyman ethic, and describes a light fixture he saw at the bank. They break bread.

"How are you, Angel?"

"Getting used to the pinstripes."

Angel shows the inside lining of his double-breasted jacket.

"Very dapper."

"Oui, il a l'air très professionnel. Un beau politician," noted Inès.

"I think I would prefer a bunny hug of kangaroo top."

"Kangaroo? Ah... le jumper...." Baptiste crosses his arms in consternation.

"Let's have some shots."

"Bien oui, pour toi, Angel," Inès demonstrates a sense of fun that is unfamiliar to Baptiste.

They decide to go out for a stroll around the neighborhood. Inès sees a café she wants to visit.

"On peut aller au café?"

"Bien oui."

"J'ai tombé pour toi."

"What did you say?"

Angel is mad with confusion and tries to find some stability to tell Inès how he really feels. Baptiste exits the café and holds a tray of drinks and some biscotti. Angel tries to help Baptiste, but he appears to have it under control.

Angel noses his words back at Baptiste, but politely looks directly at Inès. He takes a stand. Inès puts her hands on her hips, and Baptiste knows he's pulling straws now.

"Je s'amuse."

"T'es con. He's cruel. And impolite. He barely can tell me he loves me."

Inès speaks without concern about how her words might sound.

They return to the apartment. They've all drunk too much and have lost their appetite to be with each other, save to possess anything the other person might have pinched, like a pillow or comforter.

*

They wake up early the next morning. And methodically make amends: a table is made, replete with bagels, cheese, yogurt, and fresh fruit. Fresh coffee.

Somehow everyone manages to get ready for the day. Angel sits in the front room, the curtains open, the sun splashing on the scratched hardwood floors. She falls backward like the Kool-Aid character into Angel's lap. For a moment they act deliberate, and even Baptiste admits he's in a rather awkward situation.

"Je kiffe d'aller au cinéma," said Inès.

Baptiste pours a cup of coffee and begins to show signs of disrepair in their relationship.

"What?"

"She gets into these moods! Do you remember *Breathless*, the Goddard film? Very French. That sulky American. I have the sulky Parisian."

Baptiste walks around the apartment with an air of impermanence.

"But you didn't kill a cop. You're just jealous." Everyone recalls the great Goddard film.

Inès stretches her arms back and looks up at the light fixture. Her lips quiver. She wears a tight sweater, ripped arms. She is beholden to Baptiste. Despite displaying all the traits of a dysfunctional relationship, they still look respectable as a couple.

"If I say, 'Can we go somewhere to make love?' will that finally make you believe me?"

Inès goes up to Angel and grabs him by the lapels. She pushes him lightly and makes him walk backwards.

"But you still have roast chicken and white wine with him later."

"Not anymore. He's a money-hungry evil—evil, evil." Inès slams her hand on the table. She holds her hand around a fist.

They meet at The Full Moon. Angel chooses a conservative look: a simple CK suit, tie, and Twin Towers tie clip. They order fish and chips. The Union Jack, the Royals, and the zest for British sport shine a little brighter tonight. Professor Luiz wears a cardigan, loose-fitting with droopy front pockets, and grey slacks.

"Whatever happens tonight, we did all we can do." Professor Luiz presses his hand against Angel's shoulder.

"All right."

"I write a rather sultry book on tax reform on the EU, and I end up teaching in one of England's finest schools. Now, we're on the brink of separating from Europe."

"Not because we hate Germans." Angel raises his eyebrows and smiles mischievously.

"That's right!"

Professor Luiz is a little irritated by Angel's German reference whenever Brexit is mentioned. But he understands Angel's question. He makes a polite face and tries to make the topic disappear as best he can. He can undress the silly quip with so many colorful things, including name dropping or dressing down Angel about his own feeling on Brexit. Instead, Professor Luiz allows the comment to linger.

"I recognize what it's done to people."

"The WTO is not going to kick the UK and let it fend for itself. Nor is it untrue that the Brits couldn't negotiate a better deal. I think we're giving the UK a better deal. I'm quite flattered by the words of some of the biggest spenders in England. They tend to think the money is going to waste on the EU. It's not every day we get to agree with billionaires, but here I think they are right. Besides, we use their products; to have an open channel about what they think on issues, it's useful ... for the world."

"I'm not putting anyone in the poorhouse. For that reason, I'll stand our ground on this one until the end."

"This was a major gamble. An ideological one, and you found some peace. Now you must fight like a rat caught in a corner for the rest of your life, explaining what we did."

"I'll be ready."

The cruel game of politics comes to a crescendo on the 23rd of June 2016, when the UK votes to either stay or leave the EU.

The voice of the Conservative party loses a bet. The loss holds a heavy burden for all UK PMs going forward.

Even Theresa May, only the second female PM cannot outmanoeuvre the urgency of Brexit. The powers that be are in the grip of a political process, and great personalities—which all countries need and like—hold no pace against the Brexit thrashing.

For Angel, the weight of history fails to resonate.

Journal entry:

We did it. I can say that I worked on a project that has consequences. I'm proud of our efforts. Soon we'll take on the Quebéc National Assembly back home. Or, the Louisiana legislature!

The link between a single ballot and a Brexit victory is finally discernable. Jeremy Bentham would be proud. Professor Luiz beams at a job well done. He sneers at the accusation of racism, or utopian dreams, or an unfair trade deal on the horizon. The people have spoken

They are executioners. They help sever the bond between the UK and the EU. It's a political coup d'état by convincing MPs of the merits of Brexit.

They are unaccountable to the public. There are no repercussions. They are the propulsion of a successful campaign, only because the machinery of politics is corrupt enough to allow two quite dissimilar men to come together for a time.

Professor Luiz and Angel—mentor and protégé—stand on the quiet street. They cast wide stares up the street into friendly distances. They toss single malt scotch from an EU-colored flask. They hold each other and twirl arm and arm on the crepuscular street. They are the poster child for those disloyal to the stubborn rules of etiquette.

They walk briskly over Tower Bridge. The lights of central London spill onto the glossy surface of the river Thames. How strange it feels to be meeting with friends in such a grand place.

"What do you say?"

"I got the breakdown. Every one of the districts we tagged, see, we win by an eyelash. We scooped the victory away from them."

"Brilliant!" Angel cheers with no reserve.

Contrary to Angel's expectations, Professor Luiz changed his tune after the referendum results.

Angel never thought they were going to stop and see each other. To the contrary, the gullible Angel believed they were gathering steam. Soon they would be partners once again and taking on issues related to a pro-Brexit vote.

*

Feeling dejected, Angel ventures to Eyes most nights (a little pub around the corner from Portcullis House), where he befriends a group of young professionals. They all tend to work in government, mostly as MPs' assistants. They are each dilly-dallying about whether to enter politics someday. The group includes Elizabeth, Lily, Arron, and Cole and they admit they are undecided politically. Truthfully, they are less interested with titles, and more interested in drinking, chatting, and sometimes whom they are sleeping with that night. They stand at the back of the pub, eat salty popcorn or pretzels, and discuss the topics of the day. Or else play a game of snooker with warped cues and chipped balls. Their conversations are not overly argumentative or complex, for that tends to happen during the workday. They discuss something where everyone can contribute. Meanwhile, Angel begins to use football metaphors whenever he speaks. He will say things like, "As soon as I see a glimmer of interest from an MP, I look for the end zone, and hopefully we make a touchdown." Or else: "When I write a speech it always feels like I am in a scramble to get out of the pocket."

"What is a pocket, Angel?" asked Arron.

"The scrum of players during a play, and so I am always desperate to find some open field and go downfield."

They were understanding towards each other in a faltering way, and yet Angel begins to feel a little claustrophobic by how trusting the group has become.

One night, Professor Luiz appears. He notices Angel immediately, and yet he stops at approaching his former colleague. To the contrary, Professor Luiz makes sure that Angel notices he is a little awkward at their chance meeting. Professor Luiz exits the pub. Angel follows the professor outside and calls his name.

"I was rather distraught at the time of that particular meeting. I mean, I was trying to find my place again. I didn't have it in me to tell Angel that the game was up, we were no longer going to be working together."

"But surely you should have known that he was waiting for you all during this time?" I asked.

"Listen, I grew up in a single mother home in Dagenham, London, and everything I've achieved in this life was earned through hard work. I was working furiously to find my feet again. We had lost all our contract work. I didn't get any calls from MPs at all during this time. The government was assuming all the responsibility of teaching everyone about Brexit anyway. We were finished. As far as I was concerned, Angel needed to get on with his life."

"But how could you think that just not talking to him was going to help?" I asked.

"Listen, I waited for calls from MPs. But nothing was coming our way. One thing led to another. The next thing I notice it's been one week since I spoke to him. Next, a month. It was just going along like that. I cannot really explain it. I regret it, but I cannot explain it."

Angel stands outside of Professor Luiz's office. He looks at the office hours schedule, or the recent publications by faculty in the political science department.

"Sir." Angel removes his hat and enters Professor Luiz's office.

"Angel?"

"We haven't spoken in so long. I was beginning to get worried." Angel accepts the invitation to sit down.

"Right then. We lost some of the contracts. I'm forced to go back to work. I have no choice."

"Oh. That sounds awfully sudden. I was waiting for you to call me. I didn't hear from you."

"I just came to the pub to let off some steam. But I needed to tell you something. I want you to get on with things. You cannot wait any further. I've made a real mess of things." Angel looks around the pub.

"By then I was using Oxy. I know that sounds strange,

but I was in a terrible place. I was on the verge of death. Quite frankly, Angel was far from my mind. In fact, I thought about him every once in a while, and I imagined he was okay since I was in such a dark place."

"I guess that makes sense."

"I was quite nearly dead. It makes sense. I knew he had money to cover the rent, and so I wasn't worried. Like I said, I was losing control."

I sit on a little white molded plastic chair and try and balance my Chinese noodles and stir-fry while I eat. Elizabeth has invited me over for supper, where she says she has other stories to share about Angel. Arron and Cole arrive later, when I am about to eat an Ambrosia salad. Elizabeth takes notes about my recommendation to include grapes the next time. As she looks at her iPhone, she appears a little miffed, as grapes are a staple ingredient in the recipe.

"You might think I am sounding rude, but he had a drinking problem. The truth of the matter is he became a little violent after a few pints," said Cole.

"Listen, this is the first time I've heard something like this." I eat most of my salad, but something doesn't sit right with me.

"Well, do you want the truth or not?"

"Yeah, of course."

"They were sitting on a patio in a pub in London and a group of young men walked in. They had just come from a football match. I think it was Arsenal or Crystal Palace. You know soccer. One of the lads had begun to chant some song. Angel took offence to it."

"In which sense?"

"In the way some hooligan reacts when someone doesn't

follow his orders." Cole takes a cup of tea from Elizabeth.

"But the others must have made it clear that it was okay."

"Not really. They were all keen to see how far things would go. They could see that Angel was drunk."

"I'm only saying this because I don't mind telling you what I found to be true."

"So, Angel got up and wanted to fight this lad?" I asked.

"I stopped it. I came in between them," said Arron.

"But the others, including the lad who was chanting, thought it was very strange. Angel recognized he was out of order," added Cole.

"He was very reflective, but it took a while," said Elizabeth.

"That's right. It always took him a little bit of time to make the connection that maybe he was in the wrong."

"How did he act when he realized he was in the wrong?" I sit back and smile at the group. I'm a little puzzled. I sense that I am becoming defensive.

"I, of course, ordered another tray of drinks. He was okay. No, he wasn't. It made him feel all right. But it was all rather pathetic," said Cole.

"But he was a bit different from everyone, no?" I asked.

"Of course," said Arron.

"I mean, he came from Canada, and he always wanted to play American football," said Arron.

"That's right. He had a bit of a dark side, however. And never mind a quick temper. I think it was rather shocking, his response to this man at the bar. That is all I can say," said Elizabeth.

Professor Luiz looks over the Thames while I drink

my coffee. He breaks the silence by asking me a question about American football. He admits he enjoys the highlights on the BBC, but does not understand the appeal, given the players are so big and slumberous. I'm not all that keen at giving an answer, given we are getting away from discussing Angel, but I am forced to say something.

"Indeed, all the players tend to act as camouflage for, hopefully, a perfect play. It's like is a little dance, outmanoeuvring your opponent, momentum-building, and high-pressure plays."

"Oh, there are all of those things, because it looks like a bunch of oversize men just pushing people around."

"Indeed, that part of the game is used to enable the great plays to happen. The offensive and defensive line players, whom you call large, play a critical part of the game: they are the enablers; they tend not to score points. But they play a huge part whenever a team wins—for the lumbering lummoxes enable the playmakers to do their thing."

"I suppose it's a matter of perception, because I was never noticing that part of the game. I see what you mean now."

There is no way one can blame the professor for what happened to Angel, nor do I think *anyone* is to blame. Indeed, the professor is so self-obsessed that he could not possibly project negative feelings onto another person. What's more, if the professor had the slightest feeling of guilt, he would also be dead by now. That is how fragile his mind works. Angel is responsible for his own death, and so the problem resides in trying to figure out why he would have done such a stupid act. The professor pursues the same line of questioning. The more he learns, the better he feels. Because, after all, he is deepening his understanding about a person's past, and everyone is owed that kind of understanding, dead or alive.

In the middle of the night, I receive a call from Leah.

"Say something," whispered Leah.

"Like what?" I turn on the bed side lamp.

"Like, how did I get your phone number?"

"Yeah." I turn on the TV and mute the sound. The sports highlights perk me up.

"Because I called your mother, and she told me which hotel you were staying at."

I ask her to hold the line. I track my memory. I realize I told Leah where my parents live.

"You told me some town in North Carolina. Sure enough, you were right: there was just one person with that name. I called them, and they told me you were busy at some hotel in London, England. They told me to say hi."

"Right. Hi, Leah."

"I wanted to see how things were going. Because we left on bad terms. I didn't want you to think badly of me."

"I don't think badly about you. I have never thought badly about you."

I never once thought highly about Leah. She has only shown me the dangers of young love, and that Angel occupies a part of her past only randomly. His memory is not important to her anymore. She is consumed with religion and Gordon. It terrifies me to think of the things she is actually saying about Angel in private. Leah's transformation, after she meets Gordon, is so extreme that it speaks volumes about the way a person's mind operates. Psychologists and brain specialists would be curious with Leah's answers. This is not a diatribe about religion, because I know very well the virtues of the Bible. However, the way Gordon and Leah act, and how they've turned on Angel, makes me wonder if religion shouldn't be off-limits for some people. In dealing with Leah, my role is mostly to save his name against the little bits of revisionism that I see every day.

For that reason, I'm willing to take Leah's calls at whatever hour it might be.

"I just wanted to tell you that Gordon and I feel a little bit victimized by your performance in Winnipeg. The last time you were in town."

"What is that supposed to mean?"

"I mean you didn't once offer to help my sister with her journalism career. I wonder, what gives about that?"

"I am seven hours ahead of you right now. It's four in the morning. I am trying to sleep." I turn off the TV.

"Okay. You've got a right to say what you like. But I just needed to get that off of my chest. Goddammit, Tony, you know what the hell I'm talking about!"

"Yes, of course." The line goes dead.

Leah's calls continue for the remainder of my time in London. The only consolation is she does not know my cell-phone number. I call my mother and, sure enough, Leah had been calling her several times a week recently.

"I don't want to be your friend, and so don't expect me to call and discuss this anymore."

"You call me *every* day, Leah."

"Yes, because you must understand that I am very sensitive to what you are writing. I want to get these things right."

The group of men who'd had a kerfuffle with Angel during the football match sit inside the bar. At the urging of Elizabeth, I decide to approach them and introduce myself. Just like the Bay City Rollers back in NYC. One of the members of the group recognizes me from an interview I did with Messi back in the day. It was enough of a reason for the group to ask for a selfie. However, I had never met Messi. Tanner, the one who had tussled Angel, admits it was actually John McEnroe that he remembers watching on YouTube.

"You want to know about the young man who died, right?" asked Tanner.

"Could be."

"I figured you were a journalist." Tanner touches the arm of his round glasses.

"I'm a novelist, actually."

"All right, well, we discussed it, and we're sorry about the manner in which the young man died. But you have to admit it was a rather disturbing image, to see him dangling from a bridge."

"Yeah, I suppose that's true."

Tanner takes me outside and lights a cigarette. "I'll be frank with you. This guy had a lot of balls to call me out one night while I'm with my mates. I remember holding him by the lapels, and there was a sense that he wanted to fight, but *really* wanted to fight, like end it right then and there."

"He was a football headcase from Canada. They fight to let off steam." I tried my best to calm the waters.

"I could tell that after a few moments. But I was paralyzed. I really thought my life was in danger. He looked deranged. But once I clued in, this is why I wanted to speak to you—he held one of the calmest demeanors I've ever seen. The difference between his anger and the calm was rather intoxicating. I remember when I let go of him because we were about to throw punches, I was already laughing. My mates were wondering why we didn't go. But I couldn't. He was poised. You could tell he was something different. It's not *A Tale of Two Cities*, but that's my story about him. It was quite interesting to see that kind of reaction in another person."

"He wasn't a psychopath?"

"Not at all, mate. I see those types all the time. He had his head on his shoulders, but he was also explosive. I can't really explain it more than that."

"Yeah." I stoked the fires with a suspicious look, just to get a reaction.

"Let me ask you something: did he leave a note?"

"No."

"You know what I think it was?" Tanner scratches his goatee.

"Go 'head."

"I think it was some love triangle. Or something like that." Tanner looks towards his friends and it's obvious he has nothing more to add.

I end up playing a game of snooker with Angel's friends. Arron asks me if someone from Canada is permitted to become prime minister of the UK. I offer a puzzled look, and with all their expertise and connections you think they would have the answer. I hold a blank stare.

"Of course, that is impossible. But he was all right— you know, if he was British, and he had another ten years of politics under his belt."

"He could speak French pretty good," said Elizabeth.

"Yeah, you never know, maybe he could have become PM one day." Cole makes an easy cross-corner pot.

"If he had married a Brit, I bet that would make him eligible," added Arron.

"I would have married him, but it sounds like he was still in love with Inès." Elizabeth sets up for an easy pot.

"Oh, he mentioned her name." I spill my beer at the mention of Inès's name.

"All the time. Loved that girl. But not much more than that. Just said that he loved her and left it at that."

"Yeah, funny thing with love, with some people. They might love someone, but they make no effort to make sure it happens."

The talk was turning a little mushy. I could tell they had no intention in ending the conversation. They begin to act a little bit arrogant about the whole affair. It's the first time during this project when I wonder what I had got myself into. Why would any of them bring up the idea of becoming PM? That is a very odd question to ask. It should not have been mentioned, even in jest. I remain seated, silent, like some lump, and they continue to talk and talk all about their silly conversation about becoming PM someday.

I look over the Thames and try and absorb as much of the history as I can.

Professor Luiz acts as if he wants to end our visit.

Angel and Professor Luiz return inside the bar. Angel orders two pints of Guinness. The two men drink their beer and laugh at a few incidents during their time together. At one point Angel goes over to his friends, and they talk for a few moments. Professor Luiz surveys the bar, and the two men catch a glance of each other from across the bar. They are friends. But they are not true friends. Angel returns to his drink and the two men exchange pleasantries, order one last round, and then they each go off into different directions.

*

Several years pass. Angel's only success so far is an inexplicable split from his friends at College London. The absence of Professor Luiz has been taxing, but one Angel reckons was the right decision.

He succeeds at finding work at different retail shops, who are glad to pay him under the table. At one shop, which specializes in camping gear, Angel sells the latest North Face jackets. It turns out his resumé is just enough to make his life intolerable, for the opportunities do not abound like he thought they would.

Hunter thinks just being in London will toss some sense into the kid. Yet an antagonized Angel senses the scenery as painful to his well-being.

"Either you get back to class. Or learn how to stretch a canvas into an octagon and get started yesterday," said Hunter.

"I had the chance to work as a consultant." Angel thinks thoughtfully about his choices so far.

"If Hockney can still paint, then you must attempt to champion the family name. Show them what we're made of."

"I don't get the Hockney reference?"

"Bloody hell, Angel! You're being an obstinate little

crab. Meanwhile, the Central Park Five continue to call me and ask about you."

"I can't take this." Angel sits up and takes the newspaper and gently taps the side table.

Angel admonishes the escalating tone of their conversations. He does not, however, want to lose contact with his uncle over something that he thinks he can reconcile. The allure of London takes over all of his senses. He's caught up in the everyday challenges of paying rent. All he seeks is a dose of domesticity once more. Hunter continues to press Angel. No matter what, these talks tend to launch Angel back to his time with Professor Luiz.

"I'm talking to Mohammad at 3 a.m. for at least one hour for the rest of my life."

Hunter tries to be funny. He shows off that he has diffused the situation with Angel's friends back in NYC. Angel acts numb at the mention of their names. He rummages for something to do in his small studio apartment.

"I'll go to the Tate tomorrow. Goodnight"

It should be a time of great flourishes, but Angel sees little change in the passing of time. He grips himself, at the recognition of the constancy of old institutions, his endeavors of the past. He does not seek truths but connections with the past and urges them to share a similar time-travel. And stubborn to leave Brexit remains with him, one of those life-changing moments, and so he continues to seek out other, similar paths.

Angel is okay financially, and the course of his life is not, say, pointless: lots of other professional avenues will emerge. Angel pokes his head into Professor Luiz's office. Professor Luiz's hair is slicked back and his moustache is unkempt, with long, bushy sideburns. Angel sits down on the flower-patterned chair.

"I thought our work was just beginning," asked Angel.

"Not really."

"But we've still got to negotiate a Brexit deal. There are people in Brussels we can still meet with."

"You want to know the truth? They are all a bunch of bottom-feeders. They take our ideas, and they make them their own. They make us believe they are our friends, and then they disappear."

"Right."

He begins to pace while he talks. Angel ignores the truths of the situation.

"Listen. We've scrapped the whole thing, because it's not sticking. They still think it's a mobility issue. Then there's Theresa May, getting slammed in the press every day. She can't bring this home, lad. We helped them to get the vote, and now we run for cover."

"You're back teaching?!" Angel stands up and he's now the one pacing back and forth in front of Professor Luiz's desk.

"And you're going back to class. Get yourself enrolled. I told them about you."

He holds the deference as long as he can. However, the facts of the case don't add up, and the recommendations seem a little underhanded. He just wants the ol' obliging Angel to get on with life. But given his fatherly, overprotective nature, it sounds a touch angry. It puts Angel in a bit of a spin.

Temple Bar includes dark ceiling beams, crown molding which includes a ledge of shiny silver hardware.

A dark patterned carpet, with red leather stretch seats, with thick curtains tightly pulled back.

A small group gathers to celebrate someone's birthday. They wear Arsenal jerseys. It puts Angel in the foreigner's spot at not completely getting the normal rendezvous.

The humorless bartender politely asks Angel to remove his Ascot cap. The UK doesn't miss a beat. What duty does Angel serve and to whom? Why the sudden urge to return to NYC, which only reminds him of misery?

But he looks untidy here and, despite some irreverence, he has lost his comfort after being surrounded by the beautiful people. He's begun to sneer his nose at academics, or even the experience at writing short, punchy, speeches.

Journal entry:

Professor Luiz made a shift in his thinking. Meanwhile, I have difficulty putting on a pair of socks.

Angel begins to recognize his disconnect from London. It's not that he doesn't understand Brexit, but he doesn't feel it like he's part of the UK. Even a tourist feels his cold.

"Have you been watching the markets, just on the car industry, since Brexit was announced? Sales are down all over the UK. We're in the toilet. What happens with all those working in the UK after Brexit? Or by contrast all the Brits living all across Europe?"

The bartender pours himself a cup of coffee.

"That's why we're drafting a Brexit exit plan."

"That's right. You come over here and think you're all

so clever. Just wait and see when Portugal decides they don't want to shelve UK products. The choice to leave? It might be the Brits' farewell song. I might be pulling bar in Regina tomorrow."

The bartender tosses his coffee in the sink and pours himself a fresh cup.

"That's right. Well, you'll need a parka." Angel reaches high and gives himself a knee slap.

"You just carry on at College London, and later take that cushy job in Paris or Stuttgart."

The bartender rolls up his sleeves and goes over to serve another customer.

*

Several weeks pass, Angel strolls along Portugal Street, when he sees Inès. His eyes follow the polished crane skyward; a new, exciting, building on the horizon. They have not seen each other for nearly two years.

Up to now, so much of his lived experience is through his bond with Professor Luiz, and Inès tends to exacerbate the fact that the relationship is in ruins. Or, it is two old friends, like the old famous British movie, who meet at a Tube station, and drop their lives for each other. The campaign toll is long and hard.

Two years is a hard lapse of time. For her beauty has grown more awesome. Your inability to meet during your time apart makes you jealous, and sad, and eager to possess her even more.

"Que fais-tu là?" asked Inès.

"Hi."

His voice quivers, and he begins to awkwardly rub his chin.

"Oh. Congratulations on Brexit."

"Professor Luiz seems to think we made a big difference." Angel shows a little fist pump.

"He's resentful that he has to teach. Anyway, Baptiste and I separated."

Angel awkwardly moves his hand over her face, fixing her hair.

"I want you to meet my best friend from Paris. Her name is Fanny. Isn't she pretty?" Inès turned and searched for Fanny, who was standing at the front of a café and now begins to walk over to Inès.

Listening to the conversation, he picks up words randomly. The company cannot be timelier, as Inès cares just enough and—as weird as it sounds—she takes great pleasure in navigating the conversation to make Angel look and feel a little better than a few minutes earlier.

Angel is not himself. The chuckles, which he politely masks, are easily smothered, entertained, as though they are something to build on. But how do these feelings become useful? He's invited to a party (he has to attend a great battle). Fanny appears. Fanny puts out her hand and they exchange bisous.

I sit in the lobby of the Resort Inn and am hypnotised by London. I think about Vicky back in Winnipeg: I sit in brown pleather booth and drink a cold Pilsner on tap. Vicky comes over and tops off my extra-crispy chicken fingers basket. How ignoble we are towards each other. How cosmopolitan it feels. The people are delirious, and charming, pleasant to the eye. The world feels bouncy. Suddenly, Fanny Couture appears, and I crush my hexagonal old-fashioned glass. Our introductions are her breasts on my ribs, using her scarf to stop my hand from bleeding.

All public appearances prove she's popular. She boasts that she once killed a man. She wears a fur, and red silk stilettos.

She hesitates and acts a little cold. I have underperformed. That is where she always leaves, and our eyes never touch again. At the little bar around the corner, we drink Glen Livet cocktails until the bar closes; I pester her with questions about Angel. She refuses to answer. She holds out like a pro athlete at the trade deadline. She's the last one with Angel.

Our first long kiss is over my head. She takes stock of our future. But only for her ledger. She casually deliberates on whether or not she likes me or not. She has affected me like no other woman I've ever met.

I schedule our meeting for 11 a.m., and they are the fussiest people imaginable. For example, Inès refuses to drink coffee from a carton box. Fanny appears in the doorway and, to my shame, skips over my electrified stare and remains frozen, as though waiting for any kind of attention.

They blame each other for Angel's death. Inès speaks to a lawyer to find out if there are any means to bring Fanny up on any charges (involuntary manslaughter) for putting Angel in a position where he might commit suicide.

Fanny defends herself by saying she cannot be responsible for the voluntary acts of another. Besides, as she points out, she has bits of shrapnel in her face, and uses painkillers and anti-depressants. Angel remains her only connection to work hard every day.

Baptiste pompously checks his email. I help Fanny

with her Patagonia vest. I tighten my eyebrows and tug at my nose. The group turns on me. Everyone feels embarrassment. A porter enters the room and pushes two tables together. He covers the table with a white tablecloth. He announces lunch will be served momentarily. I reply that I ordered Pizza Hut. He apologizes, causing foot-stomping laughter from everyone.

They are unpredictably calm, and carry on like old friends, when Inès decides to take a call on her mobile phone. She sits on a bench and crosses her legs. Inès slowly turns at Angel with a friendly wave, and also with the understanding that neither one will let the other down.

She tries to understand why they were apart for so long. That is, at one time, they were inseparable. Alas, neither one made the point to tell the other they want to commit.

Fanny looks over at Inès who sits on the bench alone and speaks on her mobile phone. Fanny turns and smiles at Angel.

"We're just friends," said Angel.

"She introduced me like you were her boyfriend."

"So, what are you doing here?" Angel tries to change the subject.

The chance of exploring his chances with Inès quickly disappears.

"Motivating the troops to join the Gilets Jaunes back in Paris."

"Oh?" Angel glances at Inès, who continues to talk on her mobile.

"The government of France increased the price of gas. Like, a lot. This is pretty big news. The average person can hardly afford to own a car. But that's just the tip of the iceberg."

Angel's inability to add to the conversation is saved by Inès's appearance.

"What are you talking about?" asked Inès.

"C'est quoi le truc entre toi et lui ?" asked Fanny.

"Moi et lui ? Bien, Angel est ma proche." Inès is a little embarrassed by the question.

"C'est pas ton mec ?"

"Eh bien ? Je ne sais pas. Je pense qu'il est gentil."

The two young women begin to laugh, admitting Inès is interested in pursuing Angel as more than just a friend. Any bystander on the Tube platform could, from a mile away, pick out the meaning of their conversation, and yet Angel remains an ambiguous character.

"I asked Angel to come to Paris with me."

"Go. We'll take things up when you come back? Will you do that for me Angel?" Inès grabs Angel's arm, and then reaches for Fanny's hand.

Inès tugs at Angel's arm after she takes a drag off her cigarette.

PARIS

November 2018

A sense of beauty and sophistication, with a touch of fashion. Oblivious towards the rest of the world. Or, finally, observe the bitter innuendo that is forbidding and easy to use by the locals.

The police wear little flat-top caps. Or the group of three or four soldiers who parade, holding an AK-47 on their chest. It feels a little like a French New Wave movie, wherein a flat grey Renault Frègate is out front waiting to whisk you into Paris. Look at the rich Arab men, with white goatees and flowing gowns made with golden threads. Or large groups of Black families, with accents from Senegal, Togo, or Cameroon.

The doors of the RER close.

At Gare du Nord, Fanny stands and studies the soccer scores. She wears a long puffy jacket, jeans, and a light blue turtleneck. Engrossing green eyes, high cheekbones, and big white teeth with tiny gaps, lips smothered in red lipstick. They hold hands until they arrive outside, and Angel stares at the row of public bikes.

Cafés and restaurants and Swiss hotels line the street. The eye focusses on the amicable pedestrian traffic. It has an open, inviting feeling: the accomplishment of being the subject of countless master shots, seen in innumerable cheap cinema houses with celestial carpets, salty popcorn and arctic-cold drinks.

They walk up the spiral staircase; Fanny takes a break ever couple of steps. The walls are covered in black and white wallpaper.

He perfects his courtesies at each angle of the apartment. He is once more conspiring with Professor Luiz. He positions himself for a night of strategies. But the sounds of John Coltrane smother whatever comes next. Fanny is preparing the guest room. Or lighting a scented candle. And tossing an Italian salad, with thick room-temperature fennel, and an extra light olive oil. Or else, asking Angel to look at the hot water heater. They accomplish a lot in a short amount of time. Angel has trouble disagreeing with Fanny now. Their relationship begets friendship, love, religion, and even some financial worries.

"It's the birthplace of Western Europe."

She has second and third helpings of sex. Fanny lives on according to her casual feelings about the meaning of sexual liberalism.

Her sense of French superiority is merely a reflection of a provincial style, and not believing somewhere else exists, save for Paris or the occasional visit into London.

Fanny is neither interested, nor willing to watch her unscripted words. She's brimming with ideas. Every encounter is a launch into something new. They are dismissive about everything, save orchestral styles of sex, and it does not end.

Angel must have known, going to Paris as a guest (ostensibly to see Paris) could turn very messy, very fast. Fanny is intellectually gifted, two hundred-plus size.

Journal entry:

I was curious to see Paris; however, I still don't

understand why Inès would recommend that I go, and not
come with me.

"Why can't we go together?"
"Because my friend has a spare room and you're not
in school."
Such beautiful opportunities to avoid death. But she
obliges his instincts. His reason smells like shit.
She eats a *croque monsieur*. She lathers strawberry
jelly all over the tops and sides. And consults Angel on
the English and French breakfast: le sucré or salé? She
spews on Paris culture—and the NY writers, whom she
sees everywhere, are refuse to her, as she must babysit
their whims. And public displays of violence? Boring!
Why bother when we can watch it in the movies, and
such nice figures performing so many delicious evils!
She reminisces about her parents, who own a small
kiosk at Marché Beauvau and sell fruit de mer. If she ever
has any troubles while growing up (teachers at the Lycée)
Fanny will prepare a basket of fruits de mer, and
everything will be perfect once more.
"I got A's because my parents gave my teachers gift
baskets full of mussels, clams, and crab."

As they leave the apartment, a high sun and a
troubling wind fill the street. The weather has no origins.
Life is begotten from a stage door, the alignment of
bumper-to-bumper traffic, or a cyclist maneuvering
through traffic.
They walk a short distance to Place-Paul Éluard,
where they lunch at Roi du Café. The corner brasserie has
a nice ambience. Friendly men stand at the back coffee
bar and read *Le Parisian*. The whip the smudgy pages,

mumbling French curses. A saucer clatters on the espresso machine; mini jets fume white steam. The atmosphere is convivial for experimental thinking.

"It's just a piece of pizza."

Angel folds the slice and takes a bite.

Fanny reaches over and takes a small sip of his beer, then wipes the lipstick from the glass.

Fanny holds her hand in front of her mouth.

"You know, you might want to try and remember some of these places we are visiting. Someday, you might be in Toledo, or Kalamazoo, or Springfield," said Fanny.

"You've named three rather cliché American cities."

"Oh, and Saint Adolphe."

"Saint Adolphe?"

"That's where my uncle lives."

Fanny reaches over and puts her finger on Angel's mouth, so he stops talking while he eats.

"You're not entitled to remember my sensual lips, you know, so remember that slice I bought you."

Angel shakes his head with embarrassment and smiles awkwardly, while Fanny refuses to even acknowledge their very private words.

"I'm mostly thinking about Inès."

"Never mind that."

It is an invitation to be closer. But Inès's name is used because that is who Angel is thinking about. But as he finishes his words, he knows that is not his intention. He is shedding something from the past. He is trying to come clean. He is, in fact, playing any game he can to get closer to Fanny. As he observes her reaction (a raised eyebrow, her discolored nose from too much makeup powder, or else her chubby wrist suffocating her Swatch band), he stretches back—but only for a moment, for he again tries to think about Inès. Yet, Fanny has made her memory impossible to appear.

"What?"

"Inès is getting her degree."

They arrive at the Hôtel de Ville metro station and venture to street level. A wave of yellow vests blocks the street: a forest of arms rises, moving at a leisurely pace. It appears rather tame with only the slightest antagonism for the possibility of violence.

Angel wears a yellow vest and a fluorescent orange tuque. Fanny wears a yellow vest, black tights, and pointy silver boots. She has trouble walking but manages to keep up. She's a part of the performance.

A group of men go over to the side of an expensive grey building, and begin to spray paint: *Les Gilets Jaunes triomphants.*

"I'm most definitely at the crossroads of something." Angel welcomes the adrenaline rush as he surveys the sea of yellow-jackets.

"It's called social unrest." Fanny stretches her fist into the air.

"I get it."

She avoids sophistry like a side dish of coleslaw. She manifests the purpose of talking about power, will, and depths of human suffering and meaning.

We are at war: I challenge her ideas and she crushes mine. I pit her against other thinkers, newspapers and magazines. She corrects my silly mistakes, citing Descartes and Leibniz, or *Le Devoir* and the *Washington Post,* and *Love, Vogue,* and *Paper.* She pulls at her lashes or yanks up her stocking and tightens her garter belt.

We meet for supper. She wears a simple pink V-neck with nothing underneath. My cheekbones hurt being with her.

I soon realize it is me who is initiating all of the silly games. I feel disarmed, sexually, in her presence. She has planned our meeting for one hundred years. She will engage me in some incoherent talk and make me feel as much like a luddite as I've ever felt. I mislead women. I hate women skilfully. An odd affectation ripens: a strange giggle that is connected to all of our conversations, proof of *her* focus and *my* lack of delivery skills.

We enter an antique store that sells marble fireplaces. Fanny rests her warm arm on the cold marble, and says she has no intention of going any further today.

"Can we have supper at least?" I ask.

"Yes, go ahead. I'll DM you."

Fanny knows Angel. He's part of her past, present, and future. The reason why we must discuss existentialism, or else the faulty interpretation about the reasons or justification for suicide. I forget about Angel. I am succumbing to her advances, and my flirtations... I reach over the table. Angel's death continues to build meaning in her life.

A vanload of *gendarmes* arrives at the Place de la Bastille. They line up, shoulder to shoulder, and face the protesters. They realize there is no kerfuffle; they separate and meddle through the crowd.

An unhinged passerby decides to make a name for himself and carry out a bucket-list item, and throws a smoke bomb at the *gendarmes*. The protesters run in all directions. The *gendarmes* engage the crowd with rubber bullets.

Fanny is all by herself when the *gendarme* acrobat finds a bystander. *Le Parisien*, who has a videographer on the scene, shows the *gendarme* on top of a two-door BMW sedan and pointing directly at Fanny. He looks down at his gun, and through the gauge he sees Fanny on the ground, surrounded by pillows of blood. He lifts his head to the heavens.

Journal entry:

Cook, clean, and run the apartment.

Angel calls Fanny's agent and explains what happened.
Fanny works for several underground fashion magazines, and sometimes covers big name shows. But mostly she seeks out talent and offers consultancy services, and shows designers how to take their art to the next level.

Angel calls her parents. Quite unexpectedly, Hugo, Fanny's dad, immediately takes Angel under his wing. An impromptu visit to the countryside follows. Hugo breeds Sheepadoodles. The kennel is a Picasso-like one room fieldstone house, occupied by about twenty or so Sheepadoodles. Mr. Clement, the neighbor from across the street, comes over each morning to open the back door and give the dogs free rein over the French garden.
"They are the only ones who live here. I could never stay overnight—I would feel like an intruder. I ask if I can use the bathroom. I must explain why I need to do the dishes," said Hugo.
Angel admits it's one of the sweetest things he has ever seen in his life.

As Angel looks around the small house, it dawns on him: Hugo provides upkeep to a dog shelter.

"I make about two thousand euro for each one," said Hugo.

"Nice." Angel nods approvingly.

"With references, of course."

Angel has finished putting away the groceries.

"Are you hungry?"

"I'm not really hungry. I think I'm just coming around to the fact I lost an eye."

"Look how casual you're acting."

"My country does care about me. I know I'm unarmed, but there's also one hundred thousand people, screaming their fucking heads off. I hope they don't miss me. Because I'm coming back with one eye."

Now she hears stories of trauma and violence, she feels less pity than before. Indeed, she has become enormously successful at negotiating a hefty interview fee. She's in talks with several luxury makeup companies to explore different cover-ups.

She no longer blames the *gendarmes*. Her focus is on gun control. To block anyone's sense of impunity when they use guns. She's undecided what to call her emotional state, given that she—above all—cherishes the freedom that endows the République. Police brutality. Excessive force. Unnecessary violence. She's angry, which she tempers. Her sense of understanding will soon overflow. She shows no signs of indignation, revenge, or building different forms of anger. Her disfigurement is a wall of political epithets.

Inès battles tears, knowing that Angel is holding back.

He's being difficult.

"I'll figure this out, okay? Just wait for me." Angel lightly taps his fist on the desk.

"Attends? C'est pourquoi il faut revenir!"

"J'sais." Angel lowers his head and no longer knows what he thinks or how he feels.

His jeans are wet from sweat. He removes his white tee and wraps it around his head, which garners some unwelcome looks. He carries plastic bags full of groceries, and some novelty items. His triceps are ripped.

He kicks a pop bottle through traffic. And googles over sad French women, who are less inhibited than some.

The sights all seem subject to an artsy opinion, to feel satisfaction, a pastiche of life: the little African travel boutique, with boat and flight fares; the tattoo shop; the grungy brasserie; or the church, very plain save for a single tile bearing the image of Jesus Christ with a crooked nose. Even the scooters zipping up the street, men in tight hoodies, and dark pants and baskets.

He walks up the long flight of stairs. He enters the kitchen. Fanny opens the shutter window, revealing pink potted flowers. She wears canvas shorts and a red tee.

"Where were you?" asked Fanny.

"Nowhere." Angel places some souvenirs on the counter.

"You were somewhere."

Fanny opens the fridge and removes a container of orange juice.

They are in mid-sentence interested in professing their love for each other. But they have been separated long enough to know it's only an infatuation. They are merely curious about the other person now. When they are apart they entertain ideas about other living arrangements. But once they are together, Angel has no resources to think of themselves apart. Fanny cannot breathe at the thought of Angel leaving the room.

"I started to walk."

Angel pours a glass of orange juice for Fanny and himself.

"Okay. Did you stop and have a coffee?"

Angel has no reservations anymore.

"I walked all the way to the Stade de France."

"I've never heard of anything so absurd."

"Yes, and every brasserie, patisserie, petit bar, bistro, and boulangerie—I passed."

Just a moment earlier they are complicit at imagining other surroundings. Next, they work tirelessly to sanitize these thoughts from their minds. They feel guilty at the thought of living apart. They have become specialists for each other's well-being.

"I thought of you."

Angel put his arms around Fanny and kisses her shoulder. Who is the unconscious one that offers him life or death?

Fanny stands out because she pursues Angel. Lust can block out a lot of stuff. But death is eternal. His lust was born of evil. Fanny still holds contempt for Angel, at his inability to defend manhood. Who bears guilt at the moment of death? Why should she feel ecstasy today for how she lives, while also reordering the reasons Angel dies?

The tiny ceiling lights are strategically placed to squeeze in every ray of light. The compact appliances, and the small laminated redwood table and stool, are as efficient as a high-end luxury sports car.

The small quarters are only sophisticated for a time, before he turns reflective. Paris's starry nights bleed for so many weary souls. The events of Tompkins Square Park?

The Black man?

A dish smashes on the floor, and Fanny asks, "Is everything is okay?"

Or maybe he can now warn his crew that the park is free of police. Carlos sees the look on his steward's face. Besides, this is a war.

"He could have chosen to be our friend and earn money for you and me. But he didn't!"

Angel rehearses different ways to admonish any connection with any windy night at Tompkins Square Park. My memories are not real. He focusses on how to make a deal with Netflix to talk about his famous uncle.

"You're coming on to me." Fanny pushes Angel away from her.

Angel removes his wallet and puts it on the side table. "No!"

"Saturday you stole my keys."

Fanny feels her face, but the pain is so severe; she looks upwards and appears on the verge of crying.

"God!"

Angel puts his arm around Fanny's shoulder.

It's a tender moment of trust. They have not felt like this before. They contrast their feelings for each other with new, awkward touches. Someone makes some new suggestion for tonight's schedule. They are effectively becoming one, and their love is becoming deeper by the minute.

"I need to do more interviews, to get my feelings right." Fanny wipes away her tears.

"The worst part is telling your mother one of her eyes is missing."

We take a boat cruise around London. We go to the West End and see *Grease*. Nothing is ever scripted. We like the nomadic style of our relationship. She grabs me as we walk past Harrods: "I need a hat!"

We make love in the changing rooms of the athletics section. The police evacuate the entire floor. Fanny opens the door and denies everything. She's having a heart attack. I saved her life.

"We've got enough audio to snuff out a Rolling Stones concert at Wembley. Don't you French girls know that you don't have any class at all!"

"Ce n'est pas vrai!"

Angel is overcome by the violence inflicted upon her. He feels a moral guilt, and that his refuge is to protect her by showing her the only way to love her absolutely is to kill himself.

Angel feels the crowds of Pacific College stadium. He sees the end zone. Fanny wears a mask. Each face in the crowd clamors and volunteers an eyebrow, nose, lips ... and are speedily censored by Fanny. Yet Fanny loves the attention, for she sees the human struggle at trying to understand her predicament, and it feels like boundless love.

Tobias is a pro-democracy protester. One of the leaders in the *Gilets Jaunes* movement. He wears tight black pants. His head is shaven. A *Gilets Jaunes* vest, with two pistols on the chest. The guns represent the spirit of France.

"Look who is here: Fanny lost her eye for our cause." Fanny looks over the crowd.

"The *Gilets Jaunes* movement began in part due to the high price of gasoline. It has turned into a human rights movement. We stand proud of our convictions and insistence on reform. Attacks on civilians merely reinforces the view that government does not care about the physical person. They are certainly not entitled a fair price on goods and services. The *Gilets Jaunes* is not a violent movement, but we will continue to fight injustice, and give social justice to the people. No one deserves to be maimed in the name of defending their country.

I meet Professor Luiz near Tower Bridge on the river Thames, and we find a row of food trucks. Professor Luiz orders a spicy Indian seafood curry. I order a chicken burger, that comes with curly fries on a homemade bun. We speak using a lot of stretches of silence, and people-watching. We are high on our weariness. I mention the murder in Manhattan. Apparently, a Londoner doesn't have the moral candor to say Angel should have done anything different.

Angel returns to London, with a greater sense of indecision. The walls of his attic apartment are painted canary yellow. He can't recall the last time he's been out to the pub. Professor Luiz stands at the top of the spiral staircase. A bead of sweat runs down the side of his face.

Angel sits down on the chair by the window, and watches the element turn fluorescent red. Professor Luiz straightens a print by Van Gogh above the couch and sits down.

Professor Luiz is a friendly man. A good witness of his times. But he has turned old very quickly, and nothing Angel can say or do will change the predicament he finds himself in.

Angel cannot utter the words.

"Come on, son. Speak up, lad. I can't bloody well make out what you're saying."

Angel remains silent.

"Listen, I've made quite the concessions for you." Professor Luiz searches for some real words to shake things up.

"I guess so."

"Never mind. You've been working odd jobs for nearly two years."

"That's right."

Finally, Angel sits back down, and turns the hourglass on the professor's table.

"I went to Paris."

"You're not part of the *Gilets Jaunes*, are you?"

It's a rather rude comment on the part of the professor.

Angel is seasoned enough to feel the unnecessary jab. But Angel also recognizes the professor's status and admits this kind of prodding is a sideways way of being polite. But Professor Luiz holds his stare, and Angel is expected to reply. As he tries to reply he realizes he cannot say anything to the professor, for he continuously ignores Angel's feelings. Angel is a C-paper answer, and his deepest thoughts are being used to fill a newspaper basket.

"I was actually quite close to them..." Angel arrogantly rubs his nails on his chest.

"Get off of it! I've locked some scholarship funds for

you."

"You did that?"

"That's right. Give me the next four and we'll get you back on your feet." Professor Luiz sits on pins and needles while waiting for Angel to respond. Angel however has lost the zest for life, and merely taps the side of the desk with indifference.

Jorge Cruz, an art history lecturer at College London, asks if we can go upstairs. Inside my cramped room, he smiles—crooked teeth—and in a cartoonish way places a bottle of whisky down on the small round table. We laugh like mad men.

He's a touch of class in a gloomy story. He wants me back at the Resort Inn, on an upholstered swivel chair by the window, to share a few drinks with a local who knows a thing or two about Angel.

"I cannot hear you very clearly." Jorge holds his hand to his ear.

Suddenly, Angel is acting reflective and eager to talk about all the books he has been reading lately. Jorge prods Angel to speak more, to get him out of his shell.

"Comparatively, say, to some of his contemporaries, it's not very inviting or likeable."

"What contemporaries are we referring to?"

"For instance, even say some of the New York School painters, like de Kooning, Jasper Johns, Frank Stella."

"Why not include Francis Bacon?"

"Oh heavens, he's sub-average." At the mention of Bacon Angel makes a funny face.

Angle smiles. A bit of satisfaction breaking ground with a new friend. But an uncertain future is too much.

Suddenly the art of talking turns into a grey unknown.

The brick walls are plastered with job announcements: flats for rent, computers for sale, cheapo grub at nearly pubs, and an open mic at a famous speakeasy.

"For what? You made a great point. There is body of work that is consistent with your line of thought. You just need to study more to figure out why you think such and such."

"Okay."

"Yes, yes, a kind of violence about their style. Very violent and disturbing to look at, I would agree. But very relevant for lots of other reasons that you don't mention. Angel, you can clearly see that, and I'm relieved you can do that."

I lean over the bed, search for my cigarettes; instead, I find her undies and a bra big enough to hold enough firewood for the centrepiece at Burning Man in the California desert.

I kiss away the incivility and discourtesy. Her face is a splatter of scars, which I suck on, in search of the stench of something neat and hospitable. Her screams frighten the front-desk clerk. She is one with me, and only solitary drinking can cure me.

The drink makes blinking hard, and she seems to move more quickly. She is more sober than ever. Her body is gargantuan, with ranges of colors and textures and sounds and undulations that I never dreamed of experiencing. I feel the mocking and the questions about her privacy take over me. It's perverse, her body, and the conflict, indignant, deprecating, but ultimately, pure rapture, and real consequences.

Upon meeting, most people dismiss Fanny. As a couple, Angel and Fanny look close and affectionate. They cross the street in front of Gare du Nord. Past the little crooked art installation. Men and women and their families, but mostly anxious young Black men, one leg against the wall and juggling cigarettes. If there's the slightest whiff of racism, you'll find an open door towards decency flung at you. It sounds off like this: "Just look at it my way, friend!" A simple and attractive logic.

They enter a Chinese greasy spoon. The discerning Chinese woman speaks in a mix of Chinese and French—enough to make any immigrant jealous. You're standing in the Shangri-La of the continent. The walls are covered in famous Chinese icons: Bruce Lee, War Kai Wong, and Weiwei holding a cat.

Everyone begins to eat. They are caught up in the atmosphere—a flutter of emotions as an Asian shrill clears the air. The clap of empty metal trays begins a new world order, of little consequence to everyone who already has the best fixings.

It begins to rain. They skedaddle back to Gare du Nord. There's a chorus of excitement at the front entrance: a mass umbrella dance.

Fanny looks adoringly at Angel, although they are both anxious to leave the conversation.

"I'm not angry, Angel. That would be counterproductive. I'll get angry, frustrated, and unable to protest—so what does that serve anyone?"

"You should be resting." Angel puts a pillow behind Fanny's back.

"You don't have to kiss me back if you don't want to."

"She knows."

Angel turns white. He's holding on for dear life.

"About what?"

"That I like you," said Fanny.

"I don't know why we have to complicate things." Angel stands up and goes over to the window.

"Listen, you came to visit me, and we shared something profound."

Angel is coming to terms with who he is. He grew up in the hurricane of a football career. The friendships and ethics one acquires in that world can be learned at the magazine rack of any 7-Eleven in about half an hour. Fanny is calling Angel's bluff, and now Angel has to look more strategically at his life. Was he being dishonest? Perhaps he was being called out about something that Fanny felt she had a right to do? Whatever the reasons, their relationship took on a new spin. Suddenly, Inès was no longer someone Angel has eyes for.

"I'm trying to support you."

"But you didn't have to come back. You know, that really messes with my emotions."

Angel is getting tired of hearing Fanny's answers. The time he cared for her after her injury is being thrown around the room. Fanny decides to bring Angel up to date about his life. He, in fact, is being given a lot more attention than most men deserve. Fanny's exceptional intelligence puts Angel in a new class. He's forced to come clean about their relationship. Because there's no other woman to run to. Fanny makes sure to show that she had no role in closing that door. Fanny feels these consequences allow Angel to look at her and admit his true love. But Angel is already about to squelch on any future plans they might have together.

"Because I give myself the right to choose what I want to do, way more than I care about what you think. But don't think you get off without owing me something. I never wanted to come between you and Inès."

ROUEN

December 2018

The group of *Gilets Jaunes* stand at the side of the road. Everyone smiles easily, drinks coffee, and take turns mounting an angry reproach as to why they are here.

The men are unshaven; the women put some final touches on a catchy sign; the children are left alone. Suddenly, the gravity of the situation erases the soft edge of community. Eventually they will block the traffic on the highway below.

He pauses for a moment at the end result. Where doubt can hurt us at this point in the political process. Finally, the almighty commitment, not understanding their quest, but a real outcome will happen, and so why are we here? At this point, any doubt of the end goal will destroy the political will.

The plans and strategies are designed to maximize the best outcomes. Angel begins to feel the burden of these measures. He pauses a moment; he repeats all the football routes in his head, or with Professor Luiz and a belligerent MP. And in repeating these truths to these people ... *it's their time to listen*! A struggle persists with the government of France. *Or am I here to foil some of Fanny's concerns? But none are mine*, Angel surmises.

The table of croissants loses its charm. We meet to prepare a sign and light a smoke before a protest. On the overpass above, the crowds get bigger and bigger, and more and more boisterous.

"So, so, so: solidarité!"

A dance erupts. The protest finds unity. They push forward, deeper into each other's desires, and in pursuit of an equal playing field. Angel sings and dances and feels safe, for he's no longer playing the lead in anyone's game.

"Quoi?" asked one of the protestors.

"L'homme s'est pendu!" said the little girl. The little girl points towards the bridge.

His arms flay at his sides, his feet form to his boots. The signal of death goes up the twirling rope. His body is heavy and has already lost its meaning. Oh, the screams, and the cries of children. Meanwhile, the men and women stomp at the disgust at being human.

One moment they focus on fighting for their rights, at the unfair price of *carburant*. Next, a little person dangles from a yellow synthetic rope, caught under the blue overpass sign: *Rouen*.

Trucks and cars honk and swerve. A police vehicle drives up the shoulder. The officer gets out his car.

"Qu'est-ce que vous dites?"

"L'homme qui tenait la pancarte a décidé de sauter." said the little girl.

"Par son cou." The little boy holds his neck.

LONDON

Hunter is the most impacted by his nephew's death. He was "mentoring" the lad. In constant talks. Orchestrating a brilliant future. Hunter goes to London. He gets into an argument with Cameron. Cameron blames Hunter for allowing Angel go to London in the first place.

Hunter goes out for drinks with his English agent.

He awakens in a dead man's bed. He's unsure how to breathe in a dead man's bed. He draws cigarette brush strokes in the ceiling. Next, he calls his brother.

"How did your son sleep with such a hard pillow?" asked Hunter.

"Never mind, just start cleaning up. Send me his belongings—we'll be there in few days."

"Right-o." Hunter turns over on his side and stares at the receiver. He gently places it back on the phone base.

Later, he finds himself standing in front of Angel's front door, with the thick black overlay against a white back, and listens to the conversation on the staircase below.

"You were eavesdropping?" I asked.

"Heavens, no. I'm an artist. We don't listen to things. It's all technique. I was merely acting as the lad would have acted. I think I owe the world that kind of decency for such a despicable thing he decided to do."

I've learned more about life following Angel's story than I would have investigating those unsolved murders in Brooklyn. And (for better or worse) I have enough quips from Hunter to last a lifetime. When I started this project, I made myself a promise: I would finish the novel. I also agreed to think deeply about all of the things I learned along the way. Whenever Hunter would make a reference to art, I knew that I was in for trouble. Because I am not an artist, or an art critic, but rather an average writer. Yet, I think I followed Angel for the same reasons that Hunter describes, namely that Angel possessed some artistic quality that superseded the everyday norm. He certainly showed it on the football field. I like to think he showed it in London, working with Professor Luiz. But, as I am average and cannot piece the meaning of what it means to be an artist, I go along and remain amazed by the kinds of things people say and do in the world. Despite all of Hunter's quirks, I trust his word. I leave it to believers to think what they want about Angel.

The couple on the floor beneath Angel's flat speak freely, leaving a trail of affection for Angel.

"The lad killed himself," said the older woman.

"Sure as hell doesn't say anything about you or me."

"It's not about you or us!" The older woman nearly drops her bag of groceries.

"I know!" The older man takes the bag of groceries.

"So, show some class. He was a decent White man."

The older man remains silent long enough to show some remorse.

"Well, he wasn't Black."

"Yeah, but I liked him more than half the times I seen him."

Hunter agrees to pay a few months' rent so he can decide what to do next. He goes through Angel's well-kept belongings. He donates most of his scholastic and literary texts. He sends Cameron and Madilyn a few pictures, and copies of some of Angel's university papers.

They meet at The Full Moon, where they act inconsolable. The staff reacts wrongly and finds their misery fascinating.

Hunter wears Yankee sweats, a warmup jacket, and a red Yankees cap. He holds a Rawlings glove. Professor Luiz did not sleep the night previous. He has taken leave from College London. He wears a tight turtleneck shirt and blue trouser. He abuses Oxy.

Hunter remains miffed as to why Angel would walk away from a painter's life. Professor Luiz recalls Angel's imagination, the politics, speech writing, hobnobbing.

"I'm not here to ruffle any feathers. I'm just trying to help my brother out. To try and an get some idea of what happened?"

"I have no bloody idea. I got him back on track with school. He goes off to Paris," said Professor Luiz.

"Did he show any signs he was depressed?" I asked.

"Of course, I took him out of university, and taught him how to write political speeches."

"But that was good?"

"Of course, it was good for the lad. I ignored him for several years. We went our separate ways, and I took my job back at College London."

"That's what we last heard." Hunter stands up and orders another round of drinks.

"I figured I had saved his life at that point. When he agreed to go back to school, it was better than a yes vote on Brexit as far as I was concerned. It might have been love."

"Love?"

"Some French lass."

*

A few days later, Cameron and Madilyn arrive in London. They each wear jeans and matching nylon jackets. They look like they'd planned a once-in-a-lifetime trip to London. Cameron carries a bag of cheap stuff they bought at Piccadilly Circus. He holds the plastic bag with two hands, and pretends he's indifferent about its contents.

Cameron and Madilyn arrive just as Sam and Izzy, Inès's husband and daughter, are leaving. The introductions on the staircase have a dark untamed air about them. But Madilyn and Cameron reject any strange atmosphere that might diminish their duty towards Angel. Inès arrives at the door, a little apprehensive, even saving some discord for Angel's parents at Angel's absence while he was in Paris. She leaves the door open and watches her hubby and Izzy stroll quietly up the street.

Angel's parents march into the rich townhouse with a glow of the naïve, and everyone feels warmed by the welcome. Inès does not discuss her ongoing court battle with Fanny.

Angel's death is rather boring. It has nothing to do with picking up a few yards. Baptiste and Inès are lovely. They don't talk about Fanny. They don't understand why he went to Paris.

It's as if Fanny does not exist. Hatred reigns over her name. But any airs of hatred withhold any insight about Angel. It dawns on me: his parents wouldn't have it any other way; Inès and Baptiste wouldn't have it any other way: it's an attempt to pull away from death.

The difficulty lies in the tension, the interplay between Fanny and Angel. Neither Inès nor Baptiste are able to make heads nor tail of it. Inès remains jealous. Baptiste does not accept Inès ever falling for Angel. It's as if Fanny does not exist.

By denying Fanny's existence, you deny Angel's decision to take his own life. Angel's trial to live is at its core about Fanny's being. And so, by ignoring Fanny, you deny any love Angel might have possessed for someone.

Baptiste appears in the doorway and tries to sabotage Inès's meeting with Angel's parents. He's drunk, and almost falls over as he storms into the living room.

"*She's* responsible for Angel's death." Baptiste shudders as he speaks.

"Go on. Leave us alone, you cruel man." Madilyn intervenes, finally speaking up for Inès.

Baptiste's face is covered in tears. He grips his face and tries to compose himself. But, because he is so arrogant, he cleans up looking like some Hollywood actor. We are all left a little embarrassed when the hero has tissues stuffed between his knuckles. Baptiste greets the lack of compassion as the great divide between the English and French. But Angel's parents are sensible enough to at least share with Angel's once-close friend that he is acting like an asshole. Baptiste, who is speechless, revels in his shame. Inès is no less guilty: she flares off nasty looks. She's even willing to slug it out with him if doesn't let go of the situation and get on with his life.

"I'm sorry."

Baptiste weeps and makes for the door. His appearance shows, yes, an almost snub at life for the rest of us at how real he acts. And, suddenly, our ideas about him change.

"He's evil."

Inès finds Baptiste's jacket and escorts him to the front door.

"He's struggling, like the rest of us. We all have our own way of coping." Madilyn takes a sip of her tea.

The Polaroid shows Fanny in a yellow lycra one-piece outfit. Angel wears a Mets cap and jeans, and his arm around her bottom. Madilyn keeps rubbing the picture, trying to erase Angel's scarlet tongue protruding from his mouth.

The short visit has already changed their minds about so many things regarding Angel's life.

They are flattered by Fanny's attention for Angel. I never felt so ashamed. I pretend not to understand. But it proves how parents know more than any of us.

They don't blame anyone. Nor do they think it's a tragedy. Angel loved Inès. Shamefully, Fanny meant nothing to him. But she turns the event at the overpass into a penultimate act. Fanny succeeds at challenging his being. If he acts out the act of making love to me, then life is no longer a game of rumors and bad choices. "I know," Angel explains. "I'm okay with this. I am!" He shows us he is all too human, and that he feels slighted somehow, and—here—there is nowhere else to run.

POSTSCRIPT

July 2020

Dear Anthony,

We want to apologize for the way we acted while you were in Winnipeg. We're all on a similar path, hopefully guided by God's eternal light. We see you as a beacon in our journey. We just want to remind you we love you. We pray for you. We also pray for Angel, the greatest football player who ever lived.

Love,
Leah and Gordon

October 2024

Dear Anthony,

I hope this note finds you well.
I found this entry in his Tom Clancy Journal:
Dad, I cannot deny the burden I feel for not helping the young man in Tompkins Square Park. I remember you telling me to leave. I believe you were telling me to help him. I did nothing. Find a way to forgive me.

Talk to you soon, son.
Cameron and Madilyn

The end.

About The Author

Jeremy Rafuse is from Canada. He was born in Toronto, grew up in Winnipeg and later Saskatoon. He also lived in Montreal. He was nominated for Best Screenplay at the Beverly Hills Film Festival three times, and was once a Quarter-Finalist at the Zoetrope Screenplay Contest. He is the author of the crime novel *280* and *The Red Zone Speeches*.

Jeremy currently lives in Paris, France, where he is completing his PhD in philosophy. He's also working on his third novel.

https://jeremyrafuse.wordpress.com/

https://www.instagram.com/jeremyrafuse.author/

www.ingramcontent.com/pod-product-compliance
Lightning Source LLC
Chambersburg PA
CBHW050740180626
46814CB00002B/838